EX L

VINTAGE CLASSICS

DEAD AND ALIVE

Ralph Hammond Innes was born in Horsham, Sussex, on 15 July 1913 and educated at Cranbrook School, Kent. He left school aged eighteen, and worked successively in publishing, teaching and journalism. In 1936, in need of money in order to marry, he wrote a supernatural thriller, *The Doppelganger*, which was published in 1937 as part of a two-year, four book deal. In 1939 Innes moved to a different publisher, and began to write compulsively, continuing to publish throughout his service in the Royal Artillery during the Second World War.

Innes travelled widely to research his novels and always wrote from personal experience – his 1940s novels *The Blue Ice* and *The White South* were informed by time spent working on a whaling ship in the Antarctic, while *The Lonely Skier* came out of a post-war skiing course in the Dolomites. He was a keen and accomplished sailor, which passion inspired his 1956 bestseller *The Wreck of the Mary Deare*. The equally successful 1959 film adaptation of this novel enabled Innes to buy a large yacht, the *Mary Deare*, in which he sailed around the world for the next fifteen years, accompanied by his wife and fellow author Dorothy Lang.

Innes wrote over thirty novels, as well as several works of non-fiction and travel journalism. His thrilling stories of spies, counterfeiters, black markets and shipwreck earned him both literary acclaim and an international following, and in 1978 he was awarded a CBE. Hammond Innes died at his home in Suffolk on 10th June 1998.

OTHER NOVELS BY HAMMOND INNES

HAMMOND INNES

Dead and Alive

VINTAGE BOOKS
London

Published by Vintage 2013

First published in Great Britain by Collins in 1946

Vintage
Random House, 20 Vauxhall Bridge Road,
London SW1V 2SA

www.vintage-classics.info

Addresses for companies within The Random House Group Limited
can be found at: www.randomhouse.co.uk/offices.htm

The Random House Group Limited Reg. No. 954009

A CIP catalogue record for this book
is available from the British Library

ISBN 9780099577799

The Random House Group Limited supports the Forest Stewardship
Council® (FSC®), the leading international forest-certification
organisation. Our books carrying the FSC label are printed on
FSC®-certified paper. FSC is the only forest-certification scheme
supported by the leading environmental organisations, including
Greenpeace. Our paper procurement policy can be found at:
www.randomhouse.co.uk/environment

Printed and bound in Great Britain by
Clays Ltd, St Ives PLC

To

DOROTHY

Six years is a long time. Please accept this as a gesture from one whom circumstances have made a rather poor husband.

Monte Aventino
Rome, 1946

CONTENTS

CONTENTS

CHAPTER ONE

TREVEDRA

As soon as she opened the door I was certain I should not have come. The little farmhouse, cream-washed against the green of the valley side and the grey granite outcrops, looked just as I had known it before. There was the same sound of running water in the rock below the rotten planks of the water wheel. There was the same smell of dung and new-mown grass. And there were spring flowers bright in the lichen-covered wall. The warmth of the setting sun swept time aside and memory took me by the hand and we came back tired and happy after a day in the sun and the sea. There would be chicken and fresh peas and new potatoes and a great bowl of Cornish cream to be eaten with whortleberry jam.

And then Mrs. Penruddock opened the door and I knew I had been a fool to come back to Trevedra. The lines of her face and the greying hair told me of the passage of the years and I remembered that Jenny would never walk with me again through the purple and gold of the slopes above the granite cliffs.

It was loneliness that held my hand as I entered that house, so packed full of memories. The dim hall was just the same—but the hat-stand was bare. It was our room that I was shown into. I went over to the window and gazed down the Rocky Valley to the sea. The land was warm in the dying sun. And I felt a desperate urgency to pick up my suitcase and run out of Trevedra—run without stopping until I was in the train and on my way back to London.

Sarah—we'd always called her Sarah—touched my arm. " How is she ? " I sensed by the sympathy in her voice that she knew.

" She's dead," I told her bleakly.

She didn't say anything. That somehow made it harder. And I felt an awful desire to put my head in her arms and cry.

Instead I said, " We weren't married when we came here. We said we were. But we weren't." I said it brutally, unsteadily—I wanted to dam her sympathy at all costs.

But all she said was, " I knew that. But you were in love. That's as good when the world is going mad and you haven't much time." The sun had gone down now and the valley was darkening with the chill of the night. A fresh breeze, tanged with the sea, blew in through the window. " Did you ever get married, Mr. David ? " she asked.

" No," I said, and turned away from the window. " No, we never got married. She married an R.A.F. officer while I was out in the Mediterranean."

I started to unpack. I had to do something.

She said, " I understand how you feel, dear. Mr. Penruddock died just two years ago. His ship went down off Anzio. It's hard to forget—this house is too full of memories."

I searched despondently for the right thing to say. But when I looked up, she had gone. The white of the bed that Jenny had slept in showed emptily in the gloom.

For supper that night there were lamb cutlets and fresh peas and new potatoes. But there was no whortleberry jam and only a small bowl of cream to go with the gooseberry tart. The room was warm with the lamplight and a blazing log fire. When she had cleared away Sarah came in and sat in the big cross-patched arm-chair and her knitting needles clicked rhythmically as I sat and smoked and stared into the flames.

I asked her who ran the farm now. " My younger son," she said. " He's over to my daughter's at Bude to-night. There's a big sale to-morrow. We could do with some calves. My eldest is still abroad. He took a regular commission. He's in China now."

" And your husband ? " I asked. " Why did he go to
sea ? "

She put down her needles and looked into the fire.
" It was after Dunkirk," she said, and her voice was soft.
" He was a sailor, not a farmer, you know. We were
married in Penzance just after the last war. I was nurse
to Mr. Cavanna's children—he had the mines out to
Redruth. My husband and I met when he was on sur-
vivor's leave. His ship was torpedoed off the Lizard. He
was first mate in those days. But by the end of the war
he had his Master's certificate and his own ship. He was
a farmer's son, but he'd run away to sea. He'd got it in
his blood.

" But then, after the war, cargoes became difficult and
at length his ship was laid up with the others. And he
came to me than and said, ' Sarah, we must go back to
the land. You'd like that, with your own house and all,
wouldn't you ? ' The youngest of Mr. Cavanna's children
was away to school then, so we came up to Tintagel and
bought this farm. Let me see now, that was in 1924. It
was good land and close to the sea—and though the sea
was in his blood he never wanted to go back.

" That is, not until Dunkirk. He was at the wireless
all day. After that he couldn't work, but wandered day
after day along the cliffs. I knew what was in his mind.
And I said, ' When are you going down to Plymouth ? '

" That made it easier for him. He had been worrying
about me and the farm. George had been in the Terri-
torials and was in Egypt. But Mervin was already working on the farm. He was sixteen. Mr. Penruddock showed
him everything, and he was away a week later. They
made him a first mate on an old tramp called the *William
Pitt*. A year later he was master of one of the new Liberty
ships and was away to North Africa, landing supplies for
the First Army. His ship was hit at Salerno the following
year. And then two months later it went down off Anzio.
They say it was a glider bomb. She was loaded with
petrol and ammunition." She sighed and began to knit
again. " There were no survivors. The Admiralty sent

me a telegram. It arrived when I was milking the cows
and I remember the poor beasts were very uncomfortable
because I couldn't go on, but went up on to the cliffs,
which I hadn't done since he'd left.

"And then a nice young man, whose family live over
by Bridgewater, came and told me all about it. He was
about your age and very awkward, poor lamb. He'd been
the skipper of a landing craft that had been unloading
my husband's ship."

Strange how the threads cross and recross on the loom
of life. "His ship was the *Black Prince*, wasn't it?"
I said.

She paused at her knitting and looked at me over her
glasses. "How did you know?" she asked.

"I was at Anzio, too," I told her. "I had one of the
landing craft. We were quite close to the *Black Prince*
when it happened—near enough for my eyebrows to be
singed by the heat, and our paintwork to be blistered.
It was quite instantaneous, you know," I added hastily.

She nodded slowly. Her gaze had wandered back to
the fire. "Yes," she said. "Yes, I know. I'm glad it was
sudden, like that. I've seen men back here—there's
young Billy Arken over to Boscastle, both legs gone
and his side and face all shattered. Better to die quickly
when the time comes. But it's hard on the ones left
behind."

The click of the needles filled the silence of the room
again. A log slipped in the grate—a momentary flame
and a shower of sparks.

"Why did you come back here, Mr. David?" she
asked. "You should have known better. Memories are
for the old. You're still a young man."

I sucked at my pipe. Hell! Why had I come back?

"I'm not quite sure," I told her. "But I think I
know. I think it is because I have lost my roots in
England and I am trying to find them again."

"Was there no other girl?"

"Yes," I said, "but——" The fire flared and the gilt
hands of the grandfather clock in the corner glinted.

" No, there wasn't—I know that now. Jenny was an impulsive creature. She was like a child with those lovely laughing eyes and mass of untidy hair. She bubbled with the joy of life. It was like a fountain that made every moment with her exciting. We hadn't known each other long when we came here. That was in July, and in August I was called up because I was in the Reserve.

" She wasn't the person to remain faithful to an absent lover long. I knew that. She wouldn't agree to an engagement. She said we'd get married as soon as I came back and the war was over. We were young and optimistic in those days. Then Dunkirk and the Battle of Britain—a young R.A.F. pilot officer : I got the news at Derna. I was an A.B. at the time in a destroyer, and we were supporting Wavell's men on their way west.

" Then we came home for a re-fit and I was up for a commission. *King Alfred*, that's the shore station for cadets, was quite near my people and I got home quite a bit. I met a girl I'd known since I was a kid—and, I don't know, she was kind and sweet and we got on well together. It was a dose of freshness and England after the Med. and we got engaged. A man needs something to anchor him when he's abroad for months on end and the war looks like going on for ever.

" In all I was the better part of a year in England. Then I was given a landing craft and in due course took it out on the North African landing. Then the Sicily show—that was when I heard from Jenny for the first time since that note at Derna telling me she was married. It was a pitiful little note—an airmail letter card telling me that her husband was dead, shot down in flames on a train-busting raid over the Pas de Calais."

The knitting needles had stopped clicking. " Was that when you realised you didn't love the other girl ? " Sarah asked.

" No," I said, " I don't think so. It was the next letter, which came a month later, I think, that told me that. It was from her mother. Jenny was dead—killed by a stray bomb in a nuisance raid on London. For some strange reason she had left me all her jewellery. I've got it in my suitcase now—little trinkets, some of them that I'd given her, some I didn't recognise, including a platinum wedding ring, and some old Scotch jewellery, stones set in solid silver, which her grandmother had given her when she was twenty-one."

" Why didn't you break off the engagement with the other girl, man, if you knew you didn't love her ? "

I shrugged my shoulders. " Because I was a long way from home, I suppose," I said. " I needed Pat. I was out there three years—Salerno, Anzio, Elba, South of France, Greece. I was thinking of home and how the cherry blossom would look on the old grey stone of the little church down by the river. You've never been to Italy, have you ? Their churches are all pretentious with stucco and baroque—like the glamorous East, there was nothing sincere about it. I longed for the plain mellow stone of England. And somehow Pat fitted into the picture."

" Then what in heaven's name are you doing down here ? "

" Oh, I don't know," I said. " Five years is a long time. In five years you form a picture, coloured by imagination. And when I came back I thought it would be like it had been with Jenny. I had told her to fix it so that we got married at a registry office right away, the day I came down, so that we could get away the same day to some quiet little country pub where I could wallow in the beauty of the country and have a wife with me.

" Instead, she meets me with her mother. Things aren't fixed. She wants a church wedding, bridesmaids and confetti. I'm to stay with my people and we're to prospect for a house. Oh, God, you've no idea ! They talked of rationing and domestic affairs. Her mother, a pleasant stupid woman, was with her all the time. A playful brother, who was something on the Urban District Council, twitted me about Signorinas. They talked of the good times we'd had in the Middle East and

Italy and of what I was going to do now—would I, who had no job and no qualifications, be able to support a wife? It was horrible. Pat was even stupid enough to suggest a honeymoon in Italy with my getting a job in U.N.R.R.A. or something. That was the end. I'd had it. I left her a note and wired you. That was yesterday morning.

"You see," I said. "I've nothing in common with them. I'm a foreigner in my own country. I came here because I have memories here—memories of something that was real. And—and somehow I knew you'd be a help. I knew I'd be able to talk to you."

"I'm glad you came, Mr. David," she said. "Now if you'll just open that cabinet over there, you'll find a decanter and some glasses."

When I had poured whisky out for both of us, she said, "There's a man down at Bossiney needs some help, I'm told. He's trying to get one of your landing craft off the rocks with local labour and he's finding it difficult. It came ashore in a gale on its way home from the Mediterranean—it must be more than a year ago. Somehow it drove straight up the cove and lodged high and dry on the rocks on the beach. You might stroll over in the morning."

"Yes," I said, "it will pass the time."

CHAPTER TWO

THE HULK IN THE COVE

IN THE morning I climbed the valley side where the short, sheep-cropped grass was thick with rock flowers and watched the long Atlantic rollers march against the grey cliffs and thunder in a roar of surf up the entrance to the valley. The wind was out of the west, about force six. It was cold and the driven spume salted my face. The whole coast beneath the lead-grey sky was surging white, and every now and then a dull boom marked a mounting plume of spray as it climbed a nearby cliff-face.

As I walked across the bluff to Bossiney I could see Barras Head and the jagged ruins of Arthur's Castle on the headland beyond. Inland, the grey slates of Tintagel sprawled at the foot of the hills.

As I topped the rise above Bossiney, I saw the Elephant Rock that guards the starboard entrance to the cove. I stopped and looked at the angry sea that tossed and fumed against the base of it. I did not see how it was possible for a landing-craft to have got into the cove—unless it were one of the little L.C.V.P.s or A.L.C.s. And Sarah had described it as a biggish craft that practically filled the end of the cove.

I came at length to the path over the cliff top and gazed down into the cove. The tide was high and filled the cove, so that the sandy bottom was a swishing surge of white surf. It looked a wicked enough spot even in that slight sea, all rocks and swirling water. And at the end of the cove, below the sweep of the valley top and the overhanging granite cliffs on the far side, was a landing-craft. It was an L.C.T., one of the Mark Fours. It was wedged sideways on the rocks, clear of the water. And it was intact.

It was quite fantastic. It seemed to fill the tiny cove and its rusty plates and flaking paintwork merged into the dark mass of the cliffs. How it had managed to get there God only knows—it was one of those freaks of the seas that sometimes happen. It must have been swept in, its flat bows aimed at the cliffs, rolling high on the top of a mountainous wave, hit a sloping rock and swung broadside on the breaking wave to lodge where it was. What a terrifying moment it must have been for the man at the helm—or had there been no one but the seas to guide it to that incredible lodgment?

The cove, as I say, was narrow. It was not more than a hundred yards across at the entrance and it narrowed all the way until the confining cliffs swept round, green with water-moss, to meet where the valley stream flowed down a dark crevice. These landing-craft tank are about 180 feet long by 36 feet wide. What had saved it, of course, was the fact that it had been empty when it drove in. The flat bottom would draw little more than 5 feet at the stern and with her double bottom and her air tank sides she would ride the back of a breaking comber like a cork. Nevertheless it was a staggering sight to see her there, propped upon the rocks like a bait to challenge the fury of the sea. Every wave that surged into the cove seemed to gather itself together before it broke, as though to say, " I'll get it this time." But though these were spring tides and it was just about at the high, only the driven spume splattered the rusty plates with water.

The sun came out as I went down the steep path and the cove was suddenly full of colour. The earth was fresh after the night mist. The sea drowned the sound of my footsteps. I was in a world of my own—a world that belonged to Jenny and me. And yet I was not sad any more.

Perhaps I sensed the hand of Fate that had brought me back to Trevedra and down to this stranded hulk on the rocks of Bossiney Cove. I like to think so. But I don't know. Certainly I did not know then as I walked down that rocky cliff path that my feet were leading me half across the world, back to the Mediterranean, to strange happenings, to danger and a life of adventure. All I knew was that in that moment there was no longer an ache at my breast. I knew nothing of Monique then, of her elfin beauty, her tragic story and the dark rackets of Naples and the bleak life on the hills beyond Tivoli. But I felt an exaltation as I went down into the cove that I had not felt since I returned to England—an interest in life that cut across the jagged edges of my memories.

It was strange. Jenny and I might have chosen any one of a thousand and more farms in which to spend that two weeks of holiday before the war. But only one of those thousand and more farmsteads was in the next valley to the stranded wreck of an L.C.T. when the war was over. And we had chosen Trevedra—and Trevedra was that one. Of such strange things is the thread of destiny woven.

I reached the beach. It was seemingly deserted. The landing craft towered above me, big in the confines of the cove. Its rusty sides broke the force of the wind and shut me off from the noise of the sea. The thick steel door was half down, held by one rusty chain—the other had snapped and the broken end hung dejectedly against the side of the ship. I climbed over the rocks and peered beneath the hull. Sand, piled up by the winter storms, had been dug away. Except for one jagged rent near the stern, the hull seemed intact. It was one of the strangest things I had ever seen. She hadn't broken her back and she was only holed in one place. She was resting fairly on flat sloping outcrops of rock.

I clambered round to the stern. The rudders were both badly buckled, but the propellers were unharmed. There was no anchor and the girders that supported the bridge and deck housings were badly buckled. The pom-poms had gone—presumably the naval authorities had unshipped them—and the mast was snapped off short. The funnel was dented and on the seaward side the bridge

was badly shattered and looked like a twisted heap of
old scrap iron.

"Hullo, there!" The call was faint, whipped away in
the wind and the roar of the sea.

I looked up. A man was seated on one of the for'ard
bollards smoking a pipe.

"Hullo," I said. "Do you allow visitors?"

He rose from his seat and came aft. He looked a wild
figure, bearded and with his long dark hair on end with
the wind. He wore a dirty polo sweater that had once
been green, and brown corduroy slacks.

He found a rope ladder and tossed it over the side.
When I climbed over the broken rail, I found him leaning
against the side of the wheel-house. He was tapping his
teeth with his empty pipe and his grey eyes, narrowed,
searched my face.

"My name is David Cunningham," I said. "I just
came over——" I stopped there for he did not seem to
be listening. He made no move to take my hand, but
stood, staring into my face.

"My luck is in," he said suddenly. "I don't know
why you came—we'll go into that later. It's like the
answer to a prayer." He took his pipe out of his
mouth and stabbed at me with the bitten stem. "The
last time I saw you," he said, "was on the beaches at
Salerno."

"On the beaches at Salerno?" I echoed in surprise.

He nodded. "I watched you come down from the
cliff top. Something about you seemed familiar. And
when you looked up at my hail—then I knew who you
were." He started filling his pipe from a coloured silk
pouch. "On the beaches at Salerno—you had a battered
old battle bowler cocked over one eye and you steered
an L.C.T. loaded with tanks straight in to my beach. I
was never more glad to see a bloke in my life."

"I remember you now," I said.

The cliffs that hung above us blurred and the thunder
of the sea merged into the crash of artillery. In my mind's
eye I saw a sandy stretch of beach backed by low cliffs.

The shattered hulk of an L.C.T. lay on its side, half sub-
merged in the surf. An A.L.C. full of shrapnel holes
and dead bodies was beached beside the wreckage
of two ducks that had gone up on mines. And peering
out of the water was the cab of a drowned Bedford
truck and the turret of a light tank. The beach was
littered with figures, some sprawled taut in the fixity of
death, others belly-flat to the scooped-out sand in the
desperate hope of life. Bullets chipped at the sea or
riccochetted, whining, off our plates. And overhead was
the constant muffled crump of airbursts from 88's high
up in the hills.

And in the midst of all that hell a young captain stood
knee-deep in the water, waving me in to the one sound
berth. I had gone in at emergency full ahead, with
the tank engines drowning the sound of the shell bursts.
I had dropped the doors as I grounded and he had
jumped the first tank as it rolled off into three feet of
water.

He gave me a cheery wave and the last I saw of him
was riding up the beach to the shelter of the cliffs and
signalling the others to follow him and his men to join
in behind the shelter of the tanks.

I had hauled off and pulled up my doors by then. And
I left that shell-torn beach just as fast as I could, thinking
that he was a very brave man who had little chance of
life.

And now here he was, shaking me by the hand and
saying, " My name is Stuart McCrae." The beard made
a difference and without a tin hat his dark hair showed
streaks of grey. He was older than I had thought.

He glanced at his watch. " It's a bit early for ' Up
Spirits ' by naval reckoning, but I've some Scotch, and
the weather and the occasion both call for it."

He led the way into the wheel-house. It was comfortably furnished with a round plain oak table of modern
design, three chairs, an easy chair, a small desk table on
which was a typewriter, a shelf of books and a big cup-
board. Two oils and the photograph of a wide-eyed, fair-

haired girl with a baby in her arms hung on the steel walls.

As he came back from the galley with glasses and a jug of water he caught me staring at the table which was charred. The chair legs also had burns. " Salvage from my London flat," he explained.

We drank in silence. _I was thinking of those years abroad and how we'd longed for our homes. And now here I was alone in a room in a farmhouse and he was living a hermit's life in the wheelhouse of a derelict L.C.T. I didn't dare ask where the girl with the child in the photograph was. I could only suspect.

" You on holiday ? " he asked suddenly.

" Not exactly," I told him. " I've just been demobilised and I'm trying to adjust myself."

He nodded. " To adjust oneself—that is the most difficult thing in the world to do when———" He laughed and it was not a pleasant laugh. " My life here is finished." He gave a shrug to his shoulders. " England is dead to me. I've seen too much and done too much, and the roots I had are no longer there." He raised his glass to me. " Here's to the New Britain ! May no one else find it as dull as I do."

" Why do you say that ? " I asked. " Here, in this country, the world is in the making. We're at the height of our power—the oldest, the most mature and the most stable of all nations of the world. We have a democracy that works and a people with a sense of responsibility to the world. And the world looks to us."

" To us ? " His brows lifted humorously. " Maybe it looks to Whitehall, to the men who have dug themselves in behind their mahogany desks and will fight to the last white man overseas—not us."

" You're bitter," I told him.

" No, not bitter." He said it thoughtfully as he refilled our glasses. " It's just that I understand things more clearly than I did. I can understand the Twenties now— the period between the wars. They lost hope of a new world when they came back from the trenches and found all the back row boys well entrenched behind red tape entanglements. They felt there was nothing that they could do but try to forget."

I didn't make a reply. There was a lot in what he said.

"In the words of the prophet—we've had it," he said. "The generations that fought won't rule this country for another twenty years. But—" and his eyes, grey flecked with green, looked straight into mine—"this country's future isn't going to be built here at home. We must go out and wrest our title to greatness from the world as the Elizabethans did. I saw enough in the Middle East and Southern Europe to realise that the great trading days are by no means over. Now you were a landing craft skipper in the Navy. Did you ever think of the possibilities of L.C.T.s on the trade routes on enclosed seas like the Mediterranean?"

He drained the remainder of his whisky at a gulp. "I came down here to adjust myself, the same as you. I started at Bude and set out with a rucksack to walk to Land's End. This is as far as I got. I heard about this old tub in a bar at Boscastle. And when I saw it, it was the end of my walking.

"She was full of water and sand—in a filthy state. And the locals, with true Cornish thoroughness for wrecking, had taken every movable fitting. There's no compass, no ropes, no bunks, the wheel has gone and even the galley stove has been filched. But—and this is what the Navy people didn't know—the skipper of this boat did a bloody good job with the engines. When I recce-ed the ship I found the engine-room full of sand and water. But under it all were great gobs of grease. The engines were thick with it. Now I've cleared the engine-room out and the old Paxmans look like new. I had them going a week ago and they ran perfectly. I've dug her out underneath with the help of a half-witted local boy and she's O.K."

"Just a moment," I said. "Does this craft belong to you or are you just doing all this for the fun of it?"

"No, she belongs to me. I bought her for a song off

the Admiralty—they were selling her as scrap and part of the agreement is that I undertake to clear her from the beach. There's nothing in the bill of sale to say that I can't remove her intact and afloat—and that's just what I intend to do. And there's nothing to say I've got to break her up and sell her for scrap—which needless to say I don't intend to do.

"Now then," he said, "would you like to come in on this. I need somebody who understands these boats. I've done a good bit of bridging and suchlike common-sense engineering jobs. But I need somebody who knows more than I do to get her off these rocks without damaging her. And when she's off, I need somebody to watch the refitting and to sail her. Have you got any money put by ? "

" A little," I said. His enthusiasm was infective.

" Right—now here's a proposition. Apart from what I paid for her I've got about £1,500. That in my opinion is not enough capital to start out on. Your help can get her off. Then when she's afloat put up what you can and we'll form a private company with the ship as its assets, and we'll split profits on say a 70-30 or 60-40 basis according to how much you put up. We can't lose on it. Afloat she'll be worth quite a bit in a foreign country."

I helped myself to another Scotch whilst I thought it out. The question was, could she be got off and floated without tearing the hull to shreds ? And how much would it cost to float her—a lot of tackle would be required.

" Let's go out and have a look at her," I suggested.

I was quite excited. It was a proposition that had definite possibilities.

The tide had ebbed back from the rocks and we could stand on the sand and get a comprehensive view of the position of the ship.

" I've thought of rigging hawsers to the rocks at each side of the entrance to the cove and winching," he said. " But there's that jagged rock by the stern—it's the one that did the only spot of damage to her hull, and she's going to slide off her lodgment right on to it. I thought of trying to lift her off with hawsers slung to the cliff on either side, but they'd never stand the strain."

" You'd never do it that way," I told him. " You need a ramp and rollers if you're going to have any chance of getting her off without damage."

" And that would cost a packet."

" Yes," I said, " if you had to build the ramps. It would be a big concreting job and it would cost a lot." My mind was suddenly made up. " How much were you reckoning to spend on floating her off ? "

He shrugged his shoulders, his hands deep in his corduroys. " I reckoned it might cost all I had. So far, all I've put into her, except for the initial purchase, is my time and the cost of this boy whose been working with me. But I'm prepared to take a chance on all I have. It's a gamble, but I've thought it out and I figure it's worth it. That's why, apart from your knowledge and experience, I need somebody with a little extra to put into the refitting."

" All right," I said. " Now supposing I said I think I can get her off without damage—would you be willing to form a private company on a fifty-fifty share basis, a proviso being that I undertake to float her and pay the cost of doing so. That's my experience and naval contacts to offset your original idea and expense in purchasing it."

He looked at me for a moment. Then he said, " Okay. We'll call that a deal. And that calls for another whisky —we may as well finish the bottle."

Well, it was settled there and then and we drew up a preliminary agreement embodying the undertakings on either side. And next day I took the train to Plymouth.

I hadn't told him that all I possessed in the world did not amount to more than just over £500. I hadn't told him how I was going to get the craft off. I didn't know. I had bluffed him into thinking that I could do it. But could I ? Supposing the Dockyards hadn't got any L.S.T.

landing pontoons ? I needed hawsers and a winch, too. Suppose they wouldn't let me borrow them ? And if I got them how was I to rig them ?

There were so many problems to solve and I thought of nothing else as the train rolled its way across the Cornish moors and into Devon.

However, my luck was in. I discovered that a man I knew was connected with Admiralty stores. I entertained him to dinner that night. He was a lieutenant-commander now. When I'd known him in the Anzio days Slater had been one of the few regular skippers in the Combined Operations outfit. I told him the whole story.

But when I explained how I intended doing it, he shook his head. " Niente pontoons, chum," he said. " They're all out in the Pacific still. Doubt whether you'd find any at Portsmouth even. What about derricks? I've got some of those and masses of steel hawsers and winches I can lend you."

" That's going to be a hell of a job," I said. " She'd most likely break her back on the rocks. Now with a pair of those pontoons and log rollers I reckoned I could have her off in no time."

" Yes, chum, but I haven't got any," he said. " If I'd got 'em I'd let you have them—but I haven't and that's all there is to it."

I felt depressed. Now that I was in danger of being unable to do what I had so glibly promised to do, it had suddenly become violently important. I arranged to come down the following morning to have a look round the yards for what I wanted and we got quietly drunk on rum and old memories of the Wavell and Montgomery campaigns.

The following morning I went all over the yards with him. Equipment of every kind was there. But no L.S.T. pontoons. I eventually decided on two small but power-fully built hand winches, two big steel jacks, six really strong steel girders twenty feet high, pulleys, chains, and great coils of wire hawser with blocks and tackles.

Slater had all the gear loaded on to an old barge.

"There's an Admiralty tug going up to Cardiff to-morrow," he said. "We'll get her to tow it up. She should be off Boscastle about 10.00 hrs. the following morning. Get one of the motor fishing boats out and take the barge in to Boscastle. And remember—I want the barge and the gear back. I like helping my pals, but not to the extent of a court-martial."

"You'll get it back within the month," I promised him. "And the old L.C.T. will be towing it."

"Like to bet on it?" he said with a grin.

"No," I told him. "But I'll buy you the biggest dinner you've ever had in your life if I get her off."

"That's a date," he said, shaking my hand. "Lots of frutti di mare, eh? Plenty lobster and Bifstek—doppio. Well, chum, I hope you do it—but I think you've taken on rather a big thing."

That was my view, but I didn't tell him so. I spent a sleepless night trying to visualise, step by step, the equipment I'd borrowed doing the job it had to do. The next morning I returned to Tintagel. I had a late lunch at the farm and then walked to Boscastle to arrange about the boat. By the time I got back it was late to go stumbling in the dark down to Bossiney, and I decided that at least I might as well have the pleasure of surprising Stuart with my borrowed tackle.

Sarah's son, Mervin, was home that night, full of talk of the sale and the five calves he'd got. But mostly he talked of sheep. They had never had sheep on the farm and he had bought a dozen lambs. He argued that the price of wool was going up and sheep were a good invest-ment. He wasn't sure of himself and was trying to justify the purchase, which he described as a bargain that it was just foolish to miss.

I sat and smoked and enjoyed his enthusiasm, glad that I too had things to plan and work for. The atmo-sphere of the farm was less of memories and more of plans and hopes for the future.

Just as I was going to bed Sarah said with a little smile, "When are you moving down to Bossiney, Mr. David?"

I laughed. "How did you know?" I asked.

"Allow an old woman's who reared three children her intuition," she said. She tapped my arm with her knitting needles. "You wouldn't have listened to Mervin's blather with such entertainment if you hadn't got plans of your own."

I nodded. "I'm glad I came," I told her. "It seems I, too, have hunches that sometimes work out. I'll be moving down there in a day or two."

I arranged for Mervin to call me when he rose the following morning and by seven-thirty I was striding along the road to Boscastle in the early sunlight. I sang nearly all the way. I was frankly excited. I hadn't planned for myself like this for more than five years. Down the valley I caught a glimpse of the sea, blue and calm. High tide was twelve-forty. With luck the barge should be unloaded and safely moored in Boscastle shortly after midnight.

The narrow, twisting street was warm and bright in the sunlight as I came down into the valley. The long elbow of the inlet that was responsible for the village looked quiet and peaceful. Fishing boats, masts bare, were moored behind the mellow stone of the two thick sea walls. The girdling hills were a riot of colour. The green between the stone outcrops was tinged with the yellow of birds'-foot trefoil and early gorse flowers.

Down by the hard Mr. Garth was getting his boat ready. He was a man of about sixty with a weather-beaten, dour face and blue eyes beneath a dark cloth cap. "I've sent my nephew up to the head yonder to watch for the tug, Mr. Cunningham," he said. "He'll signal to Garge here when it's sighted." He indicated a big clumsy-looking man who grinned up at us from the engine hatch at the mention of his name. "Meantime the missus has a Cornish pasty she'd be glad for you to try and there's a pint or two of home-brewed cider that would be the better for the drinking of it. The missus," he added as we climbed from the boat, "is main proud of her pasties. So are all the women of Boscastle, for that matter."

He led me up the hard to a little stone house set back
in a garden of flowers and vegetables. " Yes," I said, " I
remember the Cornish pasties I had in Boscastle, though
it is more than five years since I was here."

" Aye." He nodded and spat at a stone with precision.
" Thee can't beat Boscastle for pasties."

In a cool stone-flagged room full of faded photographs,
last war relics and polished Cornish stone we ate steaming
pasties and drank rough cold cider out of glazed earthen-
ware mugs. We were served by a little girl in pigtails
tied with blue ribbon. " Thee was much talked about
down at the Black Prince last night," old Garth said.
" When I told 'em wot it were you were after doing
there were much shaking of heads." He cackled. " But
I were in Navy in last war and I said whatever they
thought, I reckoned a Navy man could do it. I bet Ezra
Hislop, who has a farm over by Trafalgar, five pund
that you d do it before the autumn weather. Aye, an'
there's witnesses to that. An' there was other bets taken,
too."

" Well, I hope I don't let you down, Mr. Garth," I said.
I was feeling uneasy.

" Thee don't have to worry about that, mister. A bet
gives an old man an interest in life. An' if it's labour you
need, I can find that. There's two boys back from the
Forces with nowt to do."

He told me that one had been in the Navy and the
other had been an R.A.S.C. driver. I asked him their names
and said, " I'll come down and have a word with them
some time."

We talked about the fishing then until George came in
to say the tug was sighted. I sought out Mrs. Garth in
the big cheerful kitchen. There was the warm sweet
smell of pastry baking and she smiled and nodded her
head when I told her how good her pasties were.

The boat's engine was already running as we came out
into the dazzling sunlight of the hard. We cast off and
the protecting hills of the inlet slipped by as we chugged
through the sparkling waters.

The tug was lying-to about three or four chains off the entrance to the harbour. She slipped her tow as we came up. "Ahoy, there," came a shout over the loud hailer. "What's your name?"

"Cunningham," I shouted.

"Okay, Cunningham, here's your scrap. Slater's compliments and if it's not returned within a month he's sending a file of Marines."

"Tell him he needn't worry," I called.

"Okay. Don't get those hawsers wrapped round your neck, landlubber." And with that crack and a wave of his hand, he was off, cleaving a deep wake at his low stern.

A signal ran up on the halyards. "Good luck!" I waved acknowledgment and almost wished I was back in the Navy.

We made Bossiney just before midday and stood off for half an hour. As we drove in on the full tide I could see Stuart standing on the battered bridge of the old hulk watching us. Everything seemed possible to me then as I brought in the equipment that would have cost a lot of money to him.

We were lashed to the stern end of the barge and we drove in through calm waters at full ahead. Old Garth knew the cove, and he hugged the cliffs on the starboard side so close that I thought he'd crush his boat between them and the barge. There was a shudder, the binding ropes strained taut and then we were still, the barge firmly grounded on sand.

"Ahoy, there," I called.

Stuart clambered down to the beach and waded out to us. Several trippers were gathered on the rocks watching us. "What the hell's the barge for?" he asked, as he climbed on board, his slacks dripping water. Then he saw what was in the barge and his eyes lighted. "Where did you get it?"

"Naval Dockyards," I said. "It's on loan."

He jumped down into the boat and wrung my hand. He was as thrilled as I've ever seen a man. "Partner," he said, " I see you know your way around." He jumped on to the barge and ran his eyes over the contents. Then he looked down at us. " There appears to be some hard work ahead of us. I suggest a drink. I've scrounged a couple of bottles of Haig from the local whilst you've been away."

By two o'clock the barge was high and dry and we got to work. We rigged two of the girders upright in the sand against the side of the barge and lashed a light cross girder to them. It was then that I first realised what a help the odd tripper could be, for the girders were very heavy and the holiday makers proved only too anxious to show how strong they were. A pulley attached to the cross girder lifted the winches clear of the barge and then with a rope we pulled the whole lot over on to the sand. It took us three hours to empty the barge by this primitive method and another two hours to stow the gear clear of the tide. Smaller items such as wooden rollers, tools, locking bolts and so on that I had included we stowed on board. Slater, bless his soul, had thrown in some tins of grease, one drum of lubricating oil and five of diesel oil. Particularly I appreciated the diesel oil since it showed that he was confident that we would in fact get off.

The question of food cropped up during the stowing as we had nothing but some pasties and a jar of cider that Mrs. Garth had thoughtfully stowed in the motor boat. A young man who had been helping us in no uncertain fashion whilst his girl friend slept in the sun on a nearby rock said, " Look, if you'd care to invite us to supper with you, I'll press-gang that good-for-nothing woman over there who happens to be my fiancée into doing some cooking."

So Stuart introduced her to the galley and the larder, and by the time we were through she had a hot meal ready for us. I don't remember her surname. To us she was always just Anne. Her fiancé's name was Bill Trevor. They came down and gave us a hand quite often after that first evening and for some strange reason things always seemed to go better when Anne was around so that we came to regard her as our mascot.

After dinner we sat on the bridge drinking and singing snatches of old songs to an accordion which Stuart played, whilst the tide crept darkly up the cove. Old Garth's boat was floating shortly after eleven, just as the moon began to rise and fill the whispering cliffs with strange shadows. The old man had heard that Bill and Anne were staying at Boscastle and offered to take them in the boat. They were so keen on the idea of going back by sea in the moonlight that Bill gave me the keys of his car and asked me to park it at the farm for the night and drive over for them in the morning. I readily fell in with the idea since it would mean transport for my luggage to Bossiney. I knew that the job I'd undertaken was one that I'd got to live with.

Down on the beach I took Garth aside to settle for the hire of the boat. But when I spoke to him of it, he shook his head angrily, " Man," he said, " I've enjoyed the day. Thee's given me a change and that's as good as a holiday. I'm my own master. You'll not be spoiling it by offering me money." He gripped my elbow in a hard hand. " An' if thee's in difficulties and need men to give thee a hand, come and see me. There's plenty of us over at Boscastle who'd come for the fun of it. We're men of the sea and if it's a question of putting a boat in the water there's few of us won't give a hand."

There was nothing adequate I could say. I shook his hand. He turned quickly away and went up to Anne. A moment later he had picked her up and was wading out to the boat with her. With a tow line fixed, the barge came off the sand with barely a sound and Stuart and I watched them chugging out of the now moonlit cove with a feeling that things were going well.

It was two o'clock before I drove back to the farm, for Stuart insisted on my explaining to him how I intended getting the craft off with the tackle I had borrowed.

The next day we started on the back-breaking task of building up a boulder and sand causeway between the rocks on which she rested and the one jagged outcrop that lay between her and flat sand. When we were tired there was always some holiday-maker to take over for a short spell. In three days we'd quite altered the appearance of the end of the cove. At night I slept like a log in an iron bedstead that Sarah had insisted on lending me complete with mattress, sheets and blankets. We lived out of tins, except once when Anne came down and whilst Bill laboured furiously with the three of us—the half-wit from the village was now under contract for the hours of daylight—Anne cooked about the biggest meal I have ever seen.

By the end of the third day we stood back in the red light of a wild sunset and could see how, by raising her stern and shifting her foot by foot, we could swing her on to the flat sand without damaging her. But the sky was flecked with dirty looking cloud. " There's a break in the weather coming," I told Stuart. The weather forecast that night included a gale warning.

It was about four in the morning that I woke. The wind was roaring against the ship's sides and I could hear the crash of the rollers growing louder as the tide came up the cove. I dressed and went up on deck. Stuart joined me shortly afterwards. Intermittently the moon broke through ragged gaps in the clouds and showed us the water tossing angrily at the entrance to the cove.

" Is it going to clear ? " Stuart asked.

" No," I said. " It's going to get worse."

He nodded . " What about that ? " He indicated our three days' work with the glowing bowl of his pipe.

" We've had it," I said. " And we'll be lucky if those boulders don't smash through the plates."

We decided to batten everything down and go up to the farm. There was no point in staying on board. There was nothing we could do.

As we climbed the path to the head in the grey light

of early day it began to rain, stinging, blinding rain that whipped our faces. The tide was high and the waves were already sucking at the sand of our ramp and weeding out the smaller boulders. "By to-morrow morning," I said, "we'll not know that we've done any work at all these last few days."

CHAPTER THREE

OFF THE ROCKS

SARAH understood our mood as soon as she saw us, wet and angry, at her door. She piled the fire high, gave us a huge breakfast, and left us alone with a chess set that had belonged to her husband.

Neither of us had played chess for a long time. We played all day, while the rain lashed at the windows and the gale shook the house. We spent the night there for we knew there would be no sleep for us on board.

Next day the wind had dropped and the sun shone on a drenched world. We went back along the cliffs and saw the sea thundering at the cliffs with blows that looked like depth charges. The tide was falling. When we reached the cove it was just as I'd first seen it. Of our three days' work there was not a trace. " But what about the boulders ? " Stuart said. " Surely they haven't been sucked out to sea ? "

" Buried under the sand," I told him. " It's lucky we hadn't started shifting her."

" There is that," he agreed. " Once we do start moving her we'll have to work fast."

Two plates had been buckled and looked as though they might have sprung a leak. Otherwise she seemed none the worse. Obviously she'd weathered bigger storms during the winter.

Bill and Anne came down to commiserate with us and we drove over to Boscastle for lunch. Stuart was in a sombre mood. He seemed dispirited about the whole thing. And his mood flared dangerously at an innocent remark of Bill's, who was trying to cheer him up. " You think I'm a child to be patted on the hand and given crumbs of comfort like a bag of sticky sweets," Stuart cried, banging down his knife and fork. His voice was

tense and strained and his eyes strangely narrowed.
" When things go wrong with you, you can go crying to
Anne for comfort. But I've got no one. Nobody in the
world. All I've got to show for my life is an old landing
craft. And that's on the rocks—like my life. I'm on the
rocks. I'm no good. I'm finished. And bloody little fools
like you come with words of comfort. I don't want your
comfort. I don't want it—do you understand ? " And
he flung out of the room.

It was a side of him that I hadn't known about until
then.

There was a stunned silence. And then Bill said,
" What an extraordinary fellow ! "

I said, " Not so extraordinary." Then I asked him if
he'd been overseas.

" No," he replied. " I was in a reserved occupation—
they lowered the age just in time."

I said, " Well, Stuart was nearly four years overseas.
He was wounded twice. And I rather fancy—he hasn't
told me, but I think I'm right—that his wife and child
were killed by a flying bomb."

Anne nodded thoughtfully. " Yes, I understand now.
Those photographs—and that charred furniture. What
hell for him ! Find him a girl, David, before it drives
him crazy."

" He's trying to marry a landing craft at the moment,"
I told her. " That's why he's so upset."

After lunch I sought out old Garth and asked him
about the weather. He told me there should be at least
two weeks of fine weather now.

I made no attempt to find out where Stuart had gone.
I'd known men in his mood in the Med. He'd walk it off.
The three of us drove into Tintagel and saw a frightful
film which was made pleasant because Anne held my
hand. She was a very sweet and understanding girl. She
insisted on coming back and cooking dinner for us.

Down in the cove Stuart had already started rebuilding
the ramp.

We were up next morning at dawn and were at work

whilst the cove was still dark and sunless though the sky was blue. We decided to build the ramp of sand this time for it was difficult to find rocks. But the curve along which the stern would be shifted had to be of rocks in order to support the girders.

Stuart was in terrific form. He nicknamed the half-wit Boo, because of his goggle eyes. And for some reason the queer boy was pleased at that. Stuart drove him unmercifully. He drove the trippers too. A man had only to pause a second gazing upon our labours and Stuart, who had suddenly cultivated a broad Cornish accent, suggested that a little physical exercise would do him a power of good. They fell for it practically every time. And as soon as they'd a shovel in their hands, he'd got them. " Man, thee'll never stand it for as much as a quarter of an hour." And then when they did stand it for quarter of an hour, he'd be so full of compliments that blisters or no they just had to go on. He paced them himself or set off one against the other. And all the time he sang old sea shanties and snatches of negro spirituals. And periodically he directed a stream of curses at Boo's rhythmically swinging back. And Boo would give him a loose grin and the sand would fly from his shovel.

It was a great day and by sundown sand and boulders were piled amongst the rocks.

The next day Bill and Anne came down and Stuart even bullied Anne into taking a shovel. And for the next hour there wasn't a man in that cove who dared refuse the proferred tool. We ran short of sand as well as rocks by midday and after lunch we rigged one of the winches and, using an old piece of corrugated iron as a bull-dozing blade, ploughed fresh sand up to the edge of the ramp. Then I borrowed Bill's car and ran down into Boscastle. I was worried about the engines. I was afraid sand might have got into them and I was taking no chances of engine failure once we'd floated her. We had to get her out of that cove and into a harbour where we could tie up, for she'd no anchors and if the sea rose before we got her out of the cove she would be wrecked.

Garth told me the nearest marine engineers would be over at Newport. He saw my disappointment and said, " Remember I told thee about a boy from the Navy who was looking round for work ? I mind now that he was an engineer."

And that was another stroke of luck, for Jack Dugan had served a year in landing craft. He'd been with a rocket ship in the Normandy and Southern France landings. " I'll walk over in the morning, sir," he said.

I really felt we were getting somewhere at last.

Next morning the cove was deserted save for a few children and two girls who giggled at us from a nearby rock. All male holiday-makers seemed to have decided to boycott the place. I wasn't surprised. Their women folk were probably putting in overtime massaging their aching backs. One lone sucker appeared in the afternoon and was persuaded to hold a shovel in white hands. He leaned on it most of the time and insisted on telling Stuart all about the essay he was writing on—Life. At length, exasperated, Stuart tore the shovel from his nerveless fingers, thrust his bearded face into the face of the would-be essayist and said, " You're useless. Do you hear ?—useless. Get out."

The young man was rather surprised and slightly scared. He got out.

Dugan had arrived shortly after breakfast and he was so thrilled at the sight of the familiar old Paxmans that by nightfall he had both engines stripped. He had dinner with us that night. " They're all right," he reported. " But there's a lot of sand needs clearing out of them. And the cylinder walls are slightly scored as though they'd been run recently." He said this accusingly and Stuart admitted his guilt.

" I was so keen to see if they'd work," he explained.

" No harm done, sir," Dugan told him. " But they need a right good clean out."

" How long will that take ? " I asked.

" Two days," was his reply. " Oh, and the auxiliary

for the dynamo is okay. Strange thing, sir," he added, "the batteries look as though they're all right, too. They're not good, of course. But no sand and sea water has got into them and I reckon I might be able to give you some light to-morrow night in place of these oil lamps you're using. I took the liberty of breaking open a locker and I've found a lot more tools, some spares, including bulbs, and several rifles and revolvers and ammunition—German, I think they are. There's grenades, too. But they're pretty rusty. The water has been at them."

Before he left he gave me a long list of things that would be required.

"Good find of yours," said Stuart as we watched his flashlight moving like a will-o'-the-wisp up the path out of the cove.

"Yes," I said, "our luck's in, I think."

By lunch-time next day the ramp was complete again. The weather was set fair. In the afternoon we began running hawsers out. I had decided not to use the winches, but to work with pulleys. Bill and Anne came down and I persuaded them to go up to the farm, borrow Mervin's trailer and drive over to Camelford to get things Dugan urgently needed like distilled water, petrol, cleansing oil, gear and lubricating oils, cotton waste and a firkin of beer.

By sundown we had two hawsers out, firmly fixed round great rocks on each side of the cove near the entrance. I attached a snaffle and pulley to the hawser fixed to the side of the cove opposite the stern of the ship and slipped the chain over one of the after deck bollards. Then we went to work on the pulley chains until it was taut.

Shortly after Bill's return Jack Dugan had the auxiliary going and the lights on.

We were pretty excited that night for to-morrow was the great day—we should know whether we were going to be able to shift the deadweight of the stern with the tackle we had. I was frankly worried. The girders were strong, but the stern, which carried the two 500 h.p. engines was a hell of a weight. Stuart and I sat smoking on the deck and talking over all the possibilities long after Bill and Anne had driven off with Dugan.

They returned with him early next morning. Working with pulleys, we had already got two of the girders in position and chains slipped underneath the hull. They were as excited as we were. " If you want any help, sir," Dugan said, " give me a shout." And he disappeared down the engine-room hatch.

The method by which I had planned to move the ship was primitive and laborious, but at the same time simple. On the landward side of the stern I rigged two girders like legs astride and bolted together at the top, to which I affixed a pulley bearing a triple chain which ran beneath the hull. To the top of the girders I also fixed a rope, ran it round one of the bollards and then pushed the girders out till they slanted away from the side of the ship at an angle of about twenty degrees out of the perpendicular. On the seaward side I did the same, but the girders were planted well away from the ship's side and slanted at the same angle towards the ship. The triple chain was brought up from beneath the hull and fixed to the pulley. To the apex I fixed a second pulley and attached it to a short hawser which I ran around a big outcrop of rock on the far side of the cove. Hauling on the pulley, we made this taut. And then we did the same to the other pair of girders.

By midday everything was set for the first move.

With Stuart and Boo on the landward girders' pulley and Bill and myself on the seaward we began to put the weight of the ship on to the girders. They bedded down, grating on the rock base of this section of our ramp. Then inch by inch the stern began to lift clear of the rock on which it rested.

When the hull was six inches clear, I ordered a halt and we manned the pulleys that bore on the hawser attached to the girders on my side and also the one that bore on the long hawser that ran direct to the ship. I called Dugan up and set him to slacken off on the pulley on the landward side.

Slowly, as we hauled on the pulleys, the girders swung into the perpendicular. The stern was then two feet clear of the rock. I was scared that the tackle would break then. It wouldn't matter so much when she was fully on our sand ramp. But if she dropped two feet on to rock she'd be holed for certain.

But the tackle held. The girders gradually slanted over in our direction until at length the hull was resting on the ground again. But now she was no longer lodged on the flat rock she had rested on for nearly a year. She was on the ramp we had built. We had swung the stern just over six feet.

In a long and pompous after-lunch speech Stuart publicly presented me with a tin of bully beef in token of the company's " gratitude for my astonishing engineering feat," regretting at the same time that at such short notice they had been unable to obtain the packet of " V " cigarettes that should have accompanied the gift.

We achieved another move during the afternoon. And after tea, as we prepared for the third, the cove echoed to the stuttering roar of the starboard engine. We all gathered round the stern as Dugan set to slow ahead. The propellers turned and we knew we would be able to get out of the cove under our own steam.

We did a third move before the sun set. The stern was by then well on to our ramp and the whole hull was slanting diagonally across the end of the cove. After dinner, working by flashlight, Stuart and I rigged rope ties for'ard and the second long hawser taut to the ship. I was taking no chances with a change in the weather.

By the following evening she was off the ramp on flat sand, pointing stern first straight towards the entrance of the cove. At high tide that evening the waves were breaking against her propellers.

A day of disappointment followed. We ran the long hawsers to the capstan and short hawsers with pulleys to the bollards on either side of the stern. With two of us manning each pulley and the engines working the capstan, she refused to slide on the sand. She wouldn't even budge with rollers under the stern. She just ground them into the sand, and that with the tide lapping all round her. All we succeeded in doing was breaking one of the long hawsers.

We patched it and settled down to the laborious task of frog-marching her into the water by cradling her on the girders as we had done when shifting the stern across the ramp. The one bright spot in the whole day was that Dugan got the port engine going.

The next morning it began to blow. Dugan confirmed my view that it was blowing up dirty and we spent a back-breaking morning running out all the hawsers and rope we had to lash her into position. By midday it was blowing half a gale and the wind was roaring up the cove from the open sea. The low tide barely cleared the rocks at the entrance and the waves were breaking in a smother of spray against the Elephant Rock. As the tide thundered in, the cove was filled with a mist of driven spume—the wind whipped it off the creamy breakers and flung it in a stinging rain against our faces as we stood watching the advancing tide.

Stuart's lips mouthed curses at the elements, but the sound of his words were whipped away by the wind and given to the cliffs behind us.

High tide was shortly after five and by that time great shaggy combers, blurred in spray, were thundering on to the beach and breaking in a cascade of foam against the stern. Every time a wave broke the ship lifted, suddenly buoyant, and as the water sucked back she settled with a thud that jarred her whole frame. The long hawsers slackened and tautened with monotonous regularity as though some great giant were plucking at them as part of the orchestra of the storm. Between the breakers they whipped and thumped at the water like galvanised eels. Every now and then there was a sickening crash against the stern plates as a rock from the demolished ramp was flung against the ship.

Suddenly Stuart pointed. A great wave was piling into the entrance, gathering height as it was contained by the narrowing cliffs. We clung to the deck stanchions and watched it swirl in, its angry, wind-whipped crest jostling in a pyramid of surf. It broke, a mountain of green and white, slap against the stern. A cataract of water swept green over the ship. It hit me in the chest, winding me and wrenching at my arms. The ship bucked like a live thing. I felt one of the starboard hawsers snap and through the flurry and foam of the spent wave I caught a glimpse of the broken end of the long hawser coiling over the stack like a great snake. It hit the deck with a thud as the water began to seethe from under us. Then the ship thudded down with a hard grinding sound.

"Rock," yelled Stuart. He had a slight gash on his forehead where his head had been flung against the sides of the stanchion to which he was clinging.

No doubt about it. The sand had been sucked back from beneath the ship and we were on the rocks. The hull was grating horribly as the ship yawed to port, straining at the short hawser that was now the only hold on the starboard side.

"We must tighten that hawser," I yelled in Stuart's ear.

He nodded and we went right aft to the bollard that held the hawser. But the chain of the pulley had been ripped from the stanchion to which it had been attached. The double loop hung trailing in the surf. The next wave seemed insignificant after its predecessor, but the grating of the bottom on the rocks was a wicked grinding sound even in that pandemonium of wind and water.

I watched the surf seeth back, judged the depth to break my fall, and jumped. I caught the chain as the backwash whipped my legs from under me. Stuart landed beside me a second later and we strained like madmen at the pulley chains. The next wave swept us up the beach, wrenching at our arms. We worked frantically in the second of slack water at the height of the wave and then hung on as it surged back. Each time the ship lifted we gained a bit until at length the hawser was taut.

Battered and breathless we made a dash through the surf and gained the rocks. We were bruised, but that was all. We climbed up by the broken chain of the bow door. The worst was over now. The wave that had parted the long hawser was the top of the tide. The ship held steady. She no longer yawed. There was only the metallic crash as she hit the rocks in the backwash of each wave and soon that was muffled as sand shifted and held beneath her flat bottom.

As the tide receded we set to work to re-rig the hawser that had parted. Dugan, who insisted upon staying, fixed up a big spotlight and got the auxiliary going. By midnight the ship was firmly held again and we settled down to cold meat washed down with hot coffee laced with rum.

" Is she going to hold, do you think? " Stuart asked. His face was tired and strained and his beard caked with salt. I suppose I looked as tired, but I was more accustomed to this sort of thing.

I said, " If the wind doesn't drop she won't."

" I see."

He said nothing after that and the three of us ate in silence. I was thinking of the way the ship had lifted to each wave.

By the end of the meal my mind was made up. " If the wind does drop," I said, " we could work her quite twenty yards down the cove on the pulleys."

He glared at me. " Aren't the elements bad enough without you trying to make it worse." His voice was almost a snarl.

I said, " Listen. She's holed just below the stern. You know that. After the pasting she'd just taken, she's probably holed in other places as well. She'll float on her double bottom, but the space between is probably full of sand just now and I doubt whether we'll be able to lift the extra weight on those girders."

" All right," he said. " You go ahead. Do what you

like. I don't care. I don't care any more. Throw the
lines off and let her smash herself to bits on the rocks."

Dugan and I went up into the gale again and set to
work rigging pulleys to the ties that held the bows to the
beach. Stuart joined us shortly afterwards, working
like a man possessed, but saying nothing. The turn of
the tide came shortly after midnight. Dugan straightened
up and sniffed at the air. " Wind's going to drop," he
shouted.

I gazed down the cove, darkly mysterious in the light
of the spotlight which was flung back by the cliffs. Out
by the entrance the seas thundered in a vague blur of
white surf. But there was a new softness in the air.
" Rain," I said.

He nodded.

Within an hour the wind had died completely and it
was raining, a steady drenching rain. By then we had
rigged pulleys to all the hawsers so that they could be
operated from the deck. We had barely fixed the last
pulley when lights showed like dancing glow-worms on
the cliff-top above the cove. We watched them as they
descended towards us.

It was Garth and Bill and about half-a-dozen Boscastle
fishermen.

" We heard thee were off the rocks," said Garth. " An'
we thought maybe you'd be in difficulties."

" We've got a lorry up on the cliff-top loaded with
ropes," Bill added.

I looked out towards the incoming tide. " I think
she'll hold," I said.

" Aye," Garth nodded. " At the high there'll be a big
swell running—no more. You'll hold all right. We just
thought maybe——" He nodded his head again. " A
right seamanlike job ye've done, Mr. Cunningham."

I thanked him for coming. " It was touch and go at
one time," I said. " And I'd still be glad of your help
when the tide is in." And I told him how I planned to
use the tide to ease the ship down the cove.

We broached the firkin of beer that Bill had brought

back from Camelford. And we crowded the little wheel-house, drinking till the crash of the waves and the lift of the stern told us the tide was in again.

Outside it was daylight, grey and wet. The seas were still big and they thundered in, to roll crashing in great roars of surf on either side of the ship. But they had lost their power and no longer broke right over the stern.

With two of us to each pulley we began to work the ship out at the flood of each wave. Those on the two long hawsers' pulleys reeled the chains in, bit by bit, whilst those on the bow and short hawser pulleys eased off as required.

An hour's work and the ship was nearly twenty yards down the cove, the limit of the pulley chains, and still held fast on all sides.

Stuart cooked us all a terrific breakfast. The strained lines had disappeared from his face. He was in great spirits. Only his bloodshot eyes told the story of the night. He wouldn't allow them to leave until the firkin was empty and then played them up the cliff-path, singing until they were all singing. Their voices died away in the murmur of the receding surf. Dugan had gone with them. And we were alone. I felt very elated and very tired. We went to bed.

I woke in the sweat of a nightmare. I had dreamed that we were afloat in the cove without ties and the ship was slowly being broken up. I opened my eyes to find the sun streaming in through the open port and Stuart shaking my shoulder and offering me a cup of tea. The noise of the sea filled the stuffiness of the cabin and now and then the ship lifted and then settled gently back on to the sand of the cove.

" Afloat ? " I asked.

He nodded.

I put a pair of slacks on and went up on deck. The sea—a quiet, complacent, gentle sea—was reaching up the cove beyond the bows. There was still a swell running, but in that warm dancing sunlit scene it was difficult to recollect the wicked thundering breakers of the night.

" To-morrow," he said, and there was relief in his voice. And I agreed.

Right away we began to rerig the pulleys so that we could ease her farther out. The long hawsers we ran direct to the capstan. We rigged ropes to the short hawsers to give them extra length. And we fixed a temporary wheel. At low tide we went round the ship to see what damage had been done. A blade of the port screw was broken and the other blades bent. That was all.

Bill and Anne came over with Dugan very early the following morning. The sea was almost flat calm. " Mr. Garth says, sir, if we're in difficulties you're to send to Boscastle," Dugan told me. " He says there'll be four boats at call if you need 'em around midday."

The tide was full at a little before nine. And just after eight-thirty we felt the first jar as the stern lifted and settled back on to the sand. Dugan got the engines going. I cast off the bow lines. Bill and Boo manned the short hawsers which we had lengthened by adding ropes.

It was with a feeling of some pride that I ordered, " Let go, for'ard," and started the capstan. Stuart operated the port hawser and I handled the starboard and so we guided the ship stern first out to the entrance of the cove. It was as easy as that. In fact the whole operation took no more than ten minutes.

I dashed up to the bridge. " Let go, for'ard," I called. Then " Let go, aft." The splash of the long hawsers going overboard told me that we were on our own. Stuart went to the wheel-house as arranged. " Slow astern both," I called down the voice-pipe that connected direct to the engine-room. I felt the bite of the screws as they began to turn. " Port ten," I ordered Stuart.

The Elephant Rock slid by, peering down at us over the starboard rail. " Half-astern both." Then to Stuart, " Steady as you go."

She came out as sweet as if she'd been coming off a beach. " Half-ahead starboard." The bows came slowly round as though the coastline were marching by. " Half-

ahead both." We steamed slowly past the Rocky
Valley about a two cables'-length off shore, past the village
of Trafalgar with its squat-towered church, past the light
on the cliff-top and into Boscastle inlet.

Word of our coming had gone before us. Half the
village was out to greet us, cheering and waving as the
rusty hulk slid between the two arms of the old stone
breakwater. We tied up alongside the hard. Old Garth
was the first aboard. And there was a burly man with a
cheery grin and mud-caked gaiters with him. "This is
my friend Ezra Hislop, Mr. Cunningham," Garth said.
"He's going to present me with five pound in the bar
and you and Mr. McCrae must come along and help
drink it."

As we went down to the pub I caught snatches of
conversation—"I mind the first time I saw 'un. I
thought I was dreaming" and "I saw 'un come in. I
reckoned she'd break up in that cove"—and so on. Some
had helped the crew off. Some had put them up for the
night. Several had helped the captain to salvage things.
The pub didn't close its doors until near on four o'clock
that afternoon and there can have been few sober fishermen in Boscastle by the time it did.

We spent all next day recovering our borrowed gear in
Bossiney Cove and loading it into the barge which Garth
towed round for us. The cove looked strange without the
rusty hulk of the landing craft lodged precariously under
the cliffs.

When we got back, Dugan approached us, cap in hand
and smothered in oil. He had with him a short, power-
fully built young fellow with a mop of unruly yellow hair.
He was dressed in what had once been khaki overalls and
he too looked as though he'd bathed in the sump of a
diesel engine.

"I was thinking that now she's off the rocks you'd be
needing a crew like, sir," Dugan said.

"Wait a minute," put in Stuart. "We're not staying
in home waters. We're going to the Mediterranean."

"That's okay with me, sir." He grinned cheerfully

through the mask of oil that smeared his face. " I ain't got no ties as you might say. An' there don't seem no job for us around these parts. My mate here feels the same way."

" What's your name ? " Stuart asked Dugan's pal.

" Eric Boyd, sir."

" You're the boy that was in the R.A.S.C., aren't you ? " I asked him.

" Yes, sir. But I were in a Water Transport Company. I had charge of a schooner running cargoes between Corsica and Naples and up to Livorno for more than a year. And I was out with the boats when I was a boy."

" Speak Italian ? " Stuart asked.

" Pretty fair, sir. You had to on them schooners. There weren't nobody but yourself and a bunch of Ityes."

Stuart glanced at me. I gave a slight nod. " Right," he said. " Come and see me in the morning and we'll fix up details."

After supper that night Stuart brought out the armoury that Dugan had found. There were three Mauser rifles with a box of a thousand rounds, all tracer, two boxes of grenades and four of those little Italian Berettas complete with holsters and a hundred rounds of ammunition apiece. The rust was only surface rust. He started on the pistols. " Mighty useful find of Dugan's," he said, and you could almost hear him purr.

Two months later I was to remember his words. At the time, however, I said, " There's not a war on in the Med now."

He looked at me with that slightly humorous lift of the eyebrows. " You'd be surprised," he said. " Remember the arms that were filched from us in Egypt, North Africa and Italy. There are caches of weapons of every kind in practically every country in the Med. And we're not all that popular in some areas where there wasn't enough food. I won't be going ashore without one of these little toys tucked away in my pocket." And he tapped the pistol he was cleaning.

Whilst he worked at the weapons, we held a brief board meeting. Our salvage worries were over. We had a ship now that could move under her own steam—not a problematical hulk lying on the rocks. And our thoughts were concentrated on how to make the best use of her.

It was agreed there and then that I should run the ship. In matters of seamanship he would come under me as my Number One. But that he should fix cargoes. He'd been in a solicitor's office before the war and he was confident that he could avoid the normal pitfalls into which a one-ship concern might fall. We agreed to do the trip out with the skeleton crew of four we already possessed—Dugan and Boyd to come in on a profit-sharing basis. The rest of the crew were to be recruited in Italy where labour would go where there was food. We would sail for Plymouth as soon as I was confident the craft could make it and whilst I supervised refitting he was to go to London and get in touch with some Italian contacts he had with a view to our investing in a suitable cargo.

Two days later we said good-bye to our friends in Boscastle. We made Plymouth in just over twenty-four hours. The sea was calm and the engines ran without a hitch. Behind us we trailed our borrowed barge with the tackle that had enabled us to become a going concern.

It was the end of the first phase.

CHAPTER FOUR

OUTWARD BOUND

IT WAS a big moment for me, coming in to Plymouth
again in a landing craft. And this time I was part owner
of it. It did not belong to the Government. As soon as
we had berthed, we sought Slater out in his office.

"Ah," he said, as we were shown in by his writer,
"I've been expecting you, Cunningham, for the past
two days."

I introduced Stuart to him. "How do you mean—
you've been expecting me?" I asked.

For answer, he picked a newspaper up from his desk
and handed it to me. It was the Western edition of a
London daily and right across one of the inside pages the
heading read: Two Men Lift Landing Craft Off Rocks—
Amazing Story of Hulk Refloated. There was a picture
of the ship on the rocks at the head of the cove and another
of her steaming into Boscastle. There were pictures of
Stuart and myself and a picture of a man in a slouch hat
which seemed vaguely familiar. The story took the whole
page and in the middle was the by-line—Bill Trevor. I
recognised the man in the slouch hat then—his picture
was captioned in heavy type: And I Helped Them Do
It.

"So that's what Bill does for a living," I said, and
handed the feature across to Stuart. I remembered his
enthusiastic use of a Leica camera which he carried every-
where. The picture of us coming into Boscastle was
probably taken from a tripper. There had been plenty
of cameras clicking as we had berthed at the hard that
morning.

"I'm glad to see he had the sense not to let on where
you got the equipment from," Slater said.

I nodded. I was wondering whether the Admiralty
would try and prevent our sailing the ship and what

effect this publicity would have on our next need—a cargo. " Well, what about this dinner ? " I said. " They should be just about opening now."

" Good," he said. " Very good idea." He drove us into town and we finished up at two in the morning on board a destroyer with eggs and bacon, washed down with rum.

The next day Stuart left for London, and Dugan, Boyd and I settled down to the job of refitting. It was a job that completely absorbed me. For a month nothing else meant anything to me. And I was as completely happy as I have ever been.

No dry dock was available so we decided to fix the damaged hull plates ourselves. This suited me, for I was determined that the refit should be thorough and at the same time that it should cost as little as possible. Slater gave me every assistance. He made me free of any equipment I needed, gave me old plates and stanchions, enabled me to scrounge all the things that cost a lot if purchased new and yet are piled, rusting, in any big Navy yard—and we weren't worrying about getting second-hand stuff. All I had to buy were spares for the engines, paint and the like. He fitted me out with ropes, hawsers, an anchor, door chains and many other things, taken from wrecks and ships that had been broken up. We even managed to get a loud-hailer.

We took the old crate out of the docks and beached her on the sands of the Sound. With winches and jacks we tipped her over on to her side and by the end of three days her hull was sound, the rudders had been straightened out and the damaged screw had been exchanged.

I made a great discovery during those three days— Boyd was no mean hand at engineering. He'd had a year as a mechanic in a garage before the war and for the first three years in the Army had been driving and serviceing transport. And then, of course, in the Water Transport Company he had been the engineer on board his schooner as well as the cargo supervisor.

And so, whilst Dugan worked steadily at the engines

to get them absolutely as perfect as old engines that have seen much service and then been buried in sea and sand for a year can be, Boyd and I set to work to fix the super-structure.

Everything that was broken, bent or twisted we ripped off with an acetyline welder or axes. By the time we'd finished there was virtually nothing left of the deck-housing and bridge except the steel walls.

From that skeleton we began to build—new bridge supports were welded in, a new stack and mast rigged, a gyro compass installed, new steel ladders fitted. And then the bridge—we built that of steel plates and aft of the stack we erected a really roomy chart-house and ward-room that ran out on either side to include the wings of the bridge where the pom-poms had been. This ward-room was constructed of ferro-concrete, curved like an adobe aft to give the least possible resistance to a follow-ing sea that might sweep over the bridge. Stanchions were erected round the remainder of the bridge to carry a canvas awning to protect us from both rain and sun.

Soon after we had righted the boat and had started work on the superstructure, something happened which didn't seem important at the time and yet was strangely linked with my fortunes.

I received a package from Bill Trevor. It contained letters addressed to us care of his paper. In his letter he apologised for not having told us that he was a newspaper man and intended to use us as copy and trusted that we were not offended by anything he had written in the article. " One or two of these letters, which I have been cad enough to open, are quite intriguing. Your pictures seem to have gone over big—you'll find quite a number of girls have written asking to be included in your crew. Some have offered to put up money. And even better, some have included photographs. I like Judy—I'd sign her on as cook ! And there's a rather pathetic letter from a Mrs. Dupont. I have done a follow-up story on the spate of letters you are receiving whilst you struggle with your own refitting . . ."

That evening I read through them all. There were a hundred and twenty-four of them. I was astonished by the frankness of some, by the desire for adventure of others and by the general absence of any realisation of the cramped living conditions on board an L.C.T. And then I came to Mrs. Dupont's letter :

26, Doughty Street,
London, W.C.1
5th July.

DEAR SIRS,
I understand from Mr. Trevor's article that you will be sailing in the Mediterranean. You are both men who have seen something of the horror of war. And I think, therefore, you will understand and do me the favour I ask.

I am an Englishwoman. I married a Frenchman in 1920. I had met him when I was driving an ambulance in the last war. We had two children—a boy and then a girl. In 1940, when the breakthrough occurred, my husband sent Monique to his sister in Italy. A week later I heard that Pierre had been killed on the Meuse. Next day my husband was shot by a band of the Croix de Feu. I joined the stream of refugees to Bordeaux. And because I was English they took me off.

Since she left me in May, 1940, I have had no word of Monique. She was 16 when she went to Italy. Now she should be 22. But I don't know even if she is still alive. It is horrible not knowing what has happened to her. My husband and my son—I know about them. Monique is all I have left of my life. The thought of her has kept me going through these long weary years.

I have worked to save enough to go to Italy. But recently I was ill and a typist's savings soon disappear. I have never asked anybody to do this because I wanted to do it myself. But now I feel desperate and your pictures showed you warm-hearted, adventurous men who might be willing to do something for a stranger.

She went to Signora Marie Galliani, Via Santa

Cecilia 17, Napoli. I have written and cabled since the war—the cable came back marked "Whereabouts unknow." Attached to this letter you will find a photograph of Monique taken when she was fifteen. Please don't lose it, for it is the only one I have of her. I enclose a stamped addressed envelope—if you cannot undertake this mission for me will you be kind enough to let me have the photograph back. I would come down to see you, but the truth is that I cannot afford the fare. Will you, therefore, please take the will for the deed and let this letter plead for me as though I were speaking to you myself.

I am sorry to burden you with a request that must come at a time when you have many practical matters to deal with. But you would be doing a great kindness to a woman who has only memories for company if you would find out what has happened to Monique.

Yours beseechingly,

Emily Dupont.

Pinned to the letter was a worn and faded photograph of a long-legged girl with an oval face and eyes and mouth that had a suggestion of laughter. I stared at it for some time, seated on the half-completed bridge as the slanting rays of the dying sun threw the shadow of the ship on the wet sands. I was thinking of the docks at Naples, of the narrow dirty streets below the Castello San Elmo, of Terracina, Cassino, Formia, and all the other towns where the rubble had been ground fine in the jaws of war. This photograph might be the likeness of a beautiful girl or the memory of a skeleton buried beneath a shattered building.

I wrote to Mrs. Dupont that night and told her that I would do what I could. Then I locked the letter and the photograph away in the little jewel case that contained Jenny's trinkets.

Two days later Stuart returned, just as we were starting to mix the concrete for the wardroom. He was nervous

and excited. " Well, how did you get on ? " I asked.
" Have you got a cargo ? "

" Come into the wheelhouse," he said. From his suitcase he pulled out two bottles of Scotch. " Get one of
those uncorked," he suggested, " whilst I get the glasses
—and prepare yourself for a shock."

" Well, what is it ? " I asked, as he poured out two
stiff drinks. I was feeling worried to the depths of my
stomach. I realised then how much the ship had come
to mean to me.

" I'll tell you the worst first," he said. " I've mortgaged
the boat—£7,500. I should have wired you first. But I
had a chance to purchase some Government transport
and I didn't want to miss it. At the same time I was
able to get a lot of Bedford spares cheap, including tyres."

" You mean," I said, " we no longer own the boat."

He nodded. " But look, David," he said. " We're out
to trade, aren't we ? To start trading you must have
money and the only capital asset we had was the boat.
I know you were expecting me to arrange for a cargo—
ourselves simply to earn money as carriers. But I saw
a lot of Italians in London and they all told me the same
thing—Italy was short of transport and of spares for the
transport they had. At the end of the war they bought
up large numbers of old Army lorries, mainly Dodges
and Bedfords. Now they're needing spares and tyres to
keep them on the roads. When I heard that the Government was disposing of some W.D. transport I decided to
act at once and get in first. I bought five quite good
Bedfords and a quantity of spares. They're garaged in
a barn belonging to a friend of mine down on Romney
Marsh and I thought of sending Boyd up to get them
painted—they're in good running order, but they don't
look up to much. Now I'm convinced that I can sell
them to an Italian in London on a payment on delivery
basis. He'll also buy the spares. I reckon we'll make
about 100 per cent profit. The spares can be stowed under
the trucks and I thought we'd load the trucks with
cigarettes which are in very short supply in Italy. Now

does that sound a good proposition ? We've got to risk something if we're going to establish ourselves. And I've got the export permits."

I had to admit it sounded all right. His enthusiasm was, as always, infective. " What about payment ? " I asked. " Will they pay in sterling ? "

" No, in goods," he said. " Their difficulty is foreign exchange. If they could purchase direct they would have done so themselves long ago. That's why there is a big profit in the deal if we can barter for a cargo that we can sell. Now I thought of opening a wholesale and mail order business in London for wines and liqueurs. Vermouth, Marsala, Spumante, Grappa, Benedetto, Strega, Triple Sec, Anisette,—there'll be some good stuff produced this season and cheap." He shrugged his shoulders. " It'll be slow," he admitted. " But it'll be profitable. Over the next twelve months I figure that we've got a good chance of making a profit of something over £10,000 and at the same time of establishing a sound business."

" Sounds too good to be true," I said.

" Well, do I go ahead ? " he asked. " Or do you think of something better ? "

" You go ahead," I said. " If you're prepared to take the risk, so am I."

" Right," he said. " Now this is what I propose to do. I've found a friend of mine who's got a job he doesn't like. He has a little money put by and we'll take him into partnership on the wine side of the business, the basis being that he runs it, we supply him at cost plus carriage and we split the profit three ways. Incidentally, he's already agreed to the idea and furthermore he is prepared to quit his job forthwith and start canvassing the big grocery stores for advance orders so that we've got an idea of how it's likely to work in practice and what wines and liqueurs are preferred before we accept such a cargo in exchange for our lorries and spares."

It sounded a pretty sensible idea. I had never seen any Italian drink other than vermouth displayed in shop

windows and yet thousands of men had come back talking
of Strega and Marsala, Lacrimo Cristi and Frascati and
Aurum. Housewives were bound to fall for it.

"Another thing," Stuart said, "I've buttoned up our
agreement. We're now a private limited company. Our
capital is 10,000 fully paid £1 shares—you own 5,000
and I own 5,000. The entire share capital is represented
by one item, the ship. I've called ourselves Cunningham
and McCrae Ltd. I'll fix up the wine side of the business
as soon as I get back to London. We'll call it Fosdyk
and Coy., Ltd.—that's my pal's name—and the shares
will be in three equal lots."

The next morning he was away again, taking Boyd
with him, and Dugan and I got on with the refitting.
Within a fortnight we'd nothing to do but paint and build
in wardroom and mess fittings and bunks. When the
painting was done and I had painted the name *Trevedra*
on her sides and stern, I went down on to the sands at
high tide and took her photo with a camera I had acquired.
I wanted the picture for Sarah.

I wired Stuart that we were ready to sail when he gave
the word and then had a final orgy of spending, chiefly
on bridge equipment—an Aldis signalling lamp, a set of
flags, a megaphone, glasses, and, most expensive item
of all, radio equipment. The following day I called at
the Post Office and found Stuart's reply waiting for me.
It read—"Arrange arrival morning twenty-seventh end
coast road Littlestone dash Dungeness Ack."

I acknowledged and then returned to the *Trevedra*.
At the flood that afternoon we winched her off on the
hook which we'd carried well out several days before.
Then we slipped into the Docks and returned all the gear
we'd borrowed. We fuelled and watered and then had one
last night ashore. Slater had found me two sailors on
leave who wanted a lift along the coast and with this
temporary addition to our crew we sailed for Dungeness
the next morning.

The sea was calm and we were off Dungeness light as
the sun rose over the bows. The Bedfords were ready

waiting on the coast road just where it turns inland a
few hundred yards short of the Pilot Inn. Through the
glasses I saw Stuart coming down on to the beach waving
to me and I ran straight in, dropping the hook about half-
a-cable's length from the shore. She beached with a
grating crash. I dropped the bow door and we made fast
with ground anchors.

I said good-bye to my temporary crew and within an
hour we had four of the Bedfords, loaded to the canopy
with crates of cigarettes, stowed and lashed. The fifth
was full of spares and had to be backed-in, off-loaded and
taken back to the farm for more. She did four trips
before the barn was cleared. But at last we had her
stowed and I got the bow anchor in and raised the door.
We winched her out and when the hook was up I went
up on to the bridge and headed the ship down Channel.

Boyd was at the wheel and Stuart joined me on the
bridge. " Just been having a look round," he said. " Nice
job you've done."

I didn't say anything and nor did he after that. We
just stood and smoked, watching the water slip past and
listening to the rhythmic chug of the engines and the
slap of the waves against the blunt bows. We were both
of us feeling that life was very good. We had achieved
something. We had a ship and a cargo. The weather was
fair and we were outward bound. We were traders—
and I thought back down the long line of British traders
and felt a surge of satisfaction that I was one of them.

We got a holding chain made fast round the bow door
and double-lashed the cargo and loose gear. I was taking
no chances with the weather in the Bay of Biscay. By
sundown the Isle of Wight had disappeared in the gathering dusk from the east and we were out of sight of land,
heading for Ushant in a long Atlantic swell.

CHAPTER FIVE

TROUBLE IN NAPLES

THE WEATHER was fair and we made a steady eight knots. Dugan and Boyd split the engine-room duties and Stuart and I the watches and wheel duty. The Bay was placid and by the morning of the third day we were running down the coast of Portugal. It began to get hot.

That night there occurred something that had a bearing on what happened later. Darkness came out of a cloudless sky. Stuart and I were on the bridge, smoking and watching the stars. The sea was almost glassy and only a slight vibration and the sound of the engines told us that we were moving. The night air was warm with the promise of heat from the desert sands of Africa.

" We should pick up the light of Cape Vincent soon," I said. I switched the light on in the covered chart recess and checked our position. According to my reckoning we were due to change course in another half-hour from south to south-east to make the Straits.

" There's a ship dead ahead of us," Stuart said.

I took my head out of the recess and gazed into the starlit night. At first I could see nothing. But as my eyes became accustomed to the darkness after the glare of the chart table light, I made out the dim shape of a small ship.

" Looks like a schooner," Stuart added, passing the glasses across to me. " She's no sails and she's without lights."

I took the glasses. It was a schooner all right, of the type that do much of the coastal trade round Spain and Italy. As I watched her a froth of white appeared at her stern. She had got her auxiliary going. Sails fluttered up clothing her bare masts and drawing fitfully in the

59

light breeze. She began to move across our bows as we
bore down on her.

I edged the wheel up and the bows came round until
we were heading straight for her again. " I am closing
her to see why she is without lights," I told Stuart.

He nodded, but made no comment. He was tapping
his teeth with his pipe and gazing for'ard at the rapidly
looming shape.

When we were about a cable's-length away the schooner
suddenly stopped her engine. Her sails dropped limply
from her masts leaving them bare as they had been
before. " Stop both," I ordered the engine-room. In the
sudden quiet the sound of the water creaming before the
thrusting bows was very loud. I switched on the loud-
hailer. " Ahoy, there ! " I called . " What ship is that ? "

Back came the reply in Spanish. The voice was the
voice of a man who was very excited.

" *Perchè non avete luce ?* " I asked, trying him in simple
Italian.

There was no reply.

We were close alongside now and I switched on the
bridge spotlight. The deck of the schooner was littered
with wine barrels below the fallen sails. The captain,
short, dark-haired and thin-faced, stood at the rail
watching us intently. " *Che e vostra*—what's the word
for cargo ? " Stuart asked me.

" *Cosa portate nella barca ?* " I called out.

There followed a stream of Spanish which was quite
unintelligible. It ended with the words, " *Vino, caballero,
solo vino.*"

" *Perchè non avete la luce ?* " I demanded again.

Another flood of Spanish from which I gathered his
dynamo had broken down. But there was a gleam of
electric-light from the companion way.

" Better push on, David," Stuart said. " He's up to
no good. I'll bet it's not wine in those barrels. But it's
none of our business and even if it were we couldn't do
anything about it."

' Okay," I said. I put the microphone of the loud-hailer to my mouth. " *Accendete luce*," I said menacingly, and then to the engine-room, " Slow ahead both."

As we gathered way the sea creamed at his stern and the little schooner made off in the opposite direction. Obviously he thought we were a naval ship.

" What do you reckon he was up to ? " I asked Stuart. " He was lying about his electric light being out of order. Anyway, he had oil storm lamps which he could have lit."

Stuart shrugged his shoulders. " Contraband," he said. " Possibly arms. There must be a lot of that going on round the Mediterranean. Think of the vast quantities of arms and equipment we lost in North Africa and Italy. Incidentally," he added. " I didn't tell you, but we had an offer to go into the arms running racket ourselves."

" How do you mean ? " I asked.

" It was whilst I was up in London that first time— about the fourth day I was there. A little man came to see me in the evening. He had a bald shiny head and square features. He looked what I have no doubt he had been—a Fascist profiteer. His opening gambit was: Would we be interested in a profitable cargo ? I said, yes, but it depended on the cargo. He talked for a long time then about the advantages of the type of ship we had. ' You don't need to worry about ports,' he said. ' A firm beach, your door down and your cargo, if loaded on lorries, is away.'

" I said the matter had not escaped our notice, and his belly shook with silent laughter. I asked him what he was suggesting. He looked at me out of his little pig eyes as though calculating the best line of approach. Then he said, ' You realise, Mr. McCrae, that there is a lot of unrest in Italy—under the surface. The unruly elements of the population are intent upon destroying the new Italy that is arising from the ashes of the old. A responsible section of the people, however, are determined that this shall not happen. But the mob is armed with weapons taken from the battlefields of your Italian campaign. Fortunately for Italy we still have our men of vision. They realise that it is necessary to have arms.

The responsible section of the people cannot save the country without arms. You will be doing a great service to Italy and to your own country if you place your ship at our disposal.'

" ' You say these arms will be profitable as a cargo ? ' I said. ' Who will pay ? '

" He explained hastily that there was not the slightest cause for alarm. Apparently some of the men with vision had also had the forethought to make plenty of money.

" It was then that I told him what I thought of him. I picked the protesting little bastard up by his collar and hit him. I kept on hitting him, explaining to him about the war we'd fought in Italy and the blood we'd spilt because of Fascism. I was really mad. And then I threw him down the stairs. My landlady was most upset and I had to explain that the man was drunk."

" What was his name ? " I asked Stuart.

" That was what was so annoying," he said. " I couldn't remember it afterwards. I went for a walk along the Embankment. I tried to remember it then. But I couldn't. Anyway, it was almost certain to be false. I gave his description to Scotland Yard and they promised to notify the Italian Government of what had occurred."

I thought about what Stuart had told me a lot that night as the ship slid across the dark unruffled waters beneath the stars. I was trying to adjust myself to the idea of an Italy controlled by the Italians. When I had last been in Naples, Civetavecchia, Piambino and Livorno, there had always been units of the British Navy, British and American M.P.s—the streets had been crowded with Allied troops. Now, of course, all that would be changed. The troops would have gone either to the Far East or back to Civvy Street or been absorbed by the armies of occupation in Germany.

I had been in Rome at the opening of the trial of Caruso, the police chief who had handed over the political prisoners to the Germans to be shot in the Ardeatine

caves. I had seen the mob surge forward in the court-
room and tear Carreta, once governor of the Regina
Coeli prison and chief witness for the prosecution, from
the hands of the Carabinieri, had seen him beaten un-
conscious, thrown from the Ponte Umberto into the
Tiber and beaten to death by oars. And I was suddenly
glad of the weapons that Dugan had found in that
locker.

Next morning we were in the Gibraltar Straits and the
steel of the deck was burning hot to the touch. There
followed four days of blazing sun and calm sea before we
raised the heat-hazed outline of the southern tip of
Sardinia. Then a breeze sprang up and held until two
days later we sighted the sugar loaf bulk of Vesuvius
crouched behind the Bay of Naples.

Boyd was on the bridge with me as we entered the Bay.
The sky and sea were very blue. Bermuda rigged
yachts heeled their white sails over against the backcloth of the city that climbed from the waterfront to the
heights on which the Castello San Elmo stood. He
pointed to the great sprawling bulk of Vesuvius. " Ever
been up to have a look at the crater, Mr. Cunningham ? "
he asked.

" No," I said. " When I arrived in Naples for the first
time the volcano had already been in eruption and it was
impossible to go up."

He nodded. " I had two months in Naples," he said.
" I was driving for a dock company. We went up
Vesuvius one Sunday from the toll road above Torre
Annunziata. Cor! What a place! I ain't ever seen
anythink like it in all my life—an' I bin ara'nd a bit.
Get Dante and Michael Angelo to team up on a kid's
idea of Hell an' it'd be a bleedin' paradise compared with
wot Vesuvius was. The sides was like a giant's castle
and when you'd got up them you was on a plateau of
black rock like metal, all smoking, and in the middle of
it was a great slag heap like a devil's dunghill. Every
thirty seconds or so there'd be a noise like a thousand tons
of bombs dropped on your feet, and the whole earth

would quiver. I went up to the top of the slag. It was hot and every time the mountain blew off it quivered like a ruddy jelly. Through gaps in the smoke I could see great red gobs of molten rock leaping out of the flames, and solidified rocks splattered the other side of the crater. I reckon she must have been throwing 'em up to near on a thousand feet. But the funnel of the crater sloped away from us otherwise we'd have 'ad it."

"Were you there when the eruption occurred?" I asked.

"Was I there! Cor, stone the crows! There—I was evacuating the women and kids from one end of Monte di Somma whilst the lava stream was swallowing it up from the other. I won't ever forget that Tuesday. There was a hell of a hailstorm at about four in the afternoon—six inches of hail in ten minutes. And half-an-hour later there was a noise like ten thousand expresses going through a tunnel and a great column of black vapour steamed up to about twenty thousand feet. It was full of ash, that vapour. It rose like a—like a huge great rolling cauliflower of muck.

"It wasn't so bad when the eruption was just a great mass of black clinkers that glowed red at night—except for the blokes whose homes were in the way of it—but when the crater started blowing off in real earnest, then I began thinking of what had happened to Pompeii.

"After that the Sangro River seemed quite tame, though I got wounded there and was downgraded. That's when I was drafted to the Water Company." He lit a cigarette. "Two months in Naples taught me a fing or two aba't huming-nature. Gor blimy, wot a place. I seen men die in the streets for lack of food. The Ityes didn't worry. The girls'd sell themselves for a tin of bully and there was gangs of hooligans on the loot. The only people wot was well fed was the boys in the Black Market. They did all right. A lot of the dock boys were in the racket one way and another. They say about a quarter of a million pounds of stuff was disappearing from the docks each month. An' I wouldn't doubt it cos

I seen drivers wiv my own eyes bring out a roll of thousand lire notes—and army pay didn't allow you saving that much, the price of vino being wot it was. An' I bet it ain't changed much."

And he was right there. Naples was the same bomb-raddled mean-streeted tart that I had known over a year ago. We berthed at the mole which the Navy had used. There was little sign of any reconstruction work. They were still using the improvised quays that we had built over sunken ships at the time of Anzio. They had cleared a few more of the shattered buildings and some wooden sheds had been erected for storage. But the port area looked just what it was—a place that had been blasted to hell from the air.

It had an air of tired lethargy about it. But then, of course, the last time I had seen it the Navy had been in charge, and despite the destruction of so much of its wharfage it had been handling a bigger volume of traffic than ever before in its history.

It was just after midday when Stuart and I went ashore. After arranging for the refuelling and watering of the ship we walked to the Banco di Napoli in the Via Roma and opened an account there. Then we went to the Zita Teresa for lunch. The long glass windows were open to the little harbour of Santa Lucia under the looming bulk of the Castello dell'Ovo. They were unloading wine casks from Ischia and the sour smell of vino was mingled with the smell of dead fish and tar. The Capri ferry was in and there was an old M.A.S. boat aground under the castle walls. They were playing *O Sole Mio* as we entered, and the man with the fiddle was the one who had played to Allied troops before the restaurant had been turned into a Men's Naafi. We had frutti di mare, ravioli, lobster salad and zabaione with Lacrimo Cristi. And the price was staggeringly cheap in comparison with what we used to pay.

After lunch we returned to the Via Roma. The firm to whom we were delivering our cargo had their offices in the Galleria Umberto. A girl with raven black hair and

D.A.

large breasts barely concealed by a low cut frock showed us in to Signor Guidici's office. "Good-afternoon, gentlemen," he said. "I have been expecting you." He was small and fat and he was smoking a cigar. He waved us to two chromium-plated chairs with a white pudgy hand. The room was expensively and uncomfortably furnished in the ultra-modern style—all steel and glass.

But he spoke English well and dealt with the matter of our cargo with dispatch. It was to be landed at Pozzuoli the following day. He had arranged registration of the vehicles and would supply drivers. When he heard that we were also carrying a cargo of five hundred thousand cigarettes he offered to buy them straight away and the price he named was good. Moreover he gave us his cheque for the full amount there and then and agreed to our terms that one truck should be retained by us until we had loaded our return cargo.

We agreed to run a similar cargo for him as soon as we had obtained the cargo we wanted for the return run. As he was showing us out he said, "There is a friend of mine who is wishing to meet you. He is hoping you will come to a little party he gives at his home to-morrow night." He went back to his desk and scribbled down the address for us. "There," he said. "It is the Villa Rosa in Posillipo. Ask for the Villa Emma—that is where Lady Hamilton entertained your Lord Nelson. The Villa Rosa is just close. There will be good wine and nice girls who speak English a little. And I think he wishes to talk about business to you."

We went out into the hot glare of the Galleria feeling pretty much on top of the world. In the space of a quarter of an hour we had settled the problem of the disposal of our cargo, had collected a cheque for nearly fourteen million lire, got an order for another cargo of a similar type, an invitation to a party and had made a new contact who wanted to do business with us. "I think this calls for a drink," Stuart said, echoing my own thoughts.

"First let's bank the cheque," I said.

He laughed. "You're more Scots than I am, I do believe, David."

We banked the cheque and then returned to the Galleria and sat in the shade of a coloured umbrella and watched the world go by, drinking cognac and lemon and discussing how best to acquire the cargo of wines and liqueurs that we needed.

A young student asked permission to sit at our table. He was thin, with slender hands, and sallow features below his dark oily hair. He spoke schoolroom English. We bought him a drink and questioned him about Italy. He told us things were very bad. The country was short of food and essential raw materials. "The men who control the country when Mussolini were Il Duce are still the masters," he said. "Many men have make much money in Black Market. They are very strong. And the people are very poor. There is not sufficient to eat and for many peoples there is no work. My father, he is a schoolteacher, and my brother, too. I am at the university. I study engineering. He gave a shrug of his shoulders and turned down the corners of his mouth. "But when I have done my examination I do not think there will be anything for me to do. There will be trouble in Italy soon," he added. "This is why Italy accepted Mussolini. We need a leader now."

He was an intelligent youth and Stuart suggested taking him along with us. He would be useful as a guide, could act as our interpreter and might know something about prices. "In the mornings I am study always at the university," he said. "But afterwards, Signori, I am free."

By the evening we had visited three or four wine dealers and had an idea at any rate of how to set about obtaining the cargo we wanted. We had also visited the post office and collected a cable from Fosdyk, setting out his requirements. It concluded with the words—"Prospects very good." On the strength of that we decided to celebrate. We took Pietro along and he showed us the cafés and wine bars of the narrow streets below the Corso

Vittorio Emanuele where the women are like the women of any big port and where men try to forget that their children are half-starving and there is no future.

I was not feeling particularly happy when we returned to the ship. The misery of the people, mingling with the fumes of the bad liquor I'd drunk, had left me depressed. Stuart morosely staggered off to bed. I made myself some tea and then, because I needed to remind myself of the fresh clean air of England, I opened my tin box and took out Jenny's jewel case. When I lifted the lid I found myself gazing at the faded photograph of a girl with pig-tails and an oval face which had a suggestion of laughter in the eyes and mouth. Monique! I had forgotten all about her and my promise to her mother. And a sudden horror seized me at all the things I'd seen that night and all the dingy hovels I had been into. Perhaps in one of those frightful little drinking dens . . . I stood the photograph on the shelf above my bed. I must find that girl—find out what had happened to her. And with this resolution I lay down on my bunk and went to sleep.

I dreamed I was being chased through horrible twisting streets. Then I was being beaten by a black-shirted hooligan because I wouldn't tell them where Monique was, and I woke to find the sun streaming in and Boyd shaking my shoulder. "Like a nice cup o' char, sir?" he asked.

I took it from him. "God! I feel lousy," I said.

"I wouldn't wonder, sir. You weren't yourself at all when you came aboard last night."

"I don't even remember coming on board," I said. I noticed with disgust that I was fully clothed.

"There's a young Itye outside, sir. Says 'e was wiv you last night an' you told him to come and see you in the morning. He don't look so good either." And he grinned.

"Oh, Pietro," I said, and sat up on the bunk. My head felt terrible. "How's Mr. McCrae?"

"Swearing somethink awful, sir."

I got to my feet and found myself looking at Monique's

photograph propped up on the shelf above my bunk.
" Send Pietro in," I told Boyd.

The boy certainly looked about as bad as I felt. He
was very white and smiled sheepishly. " Next time we
go out I take you to the good restaurant," he said.

" You're not taking me out again," I told him. Then
I gave him Monique's photograph and Mrs. Galliani's
address " Find that girl for me," I said. " And meet me
at the same table in the Galleria at three o'clock, the day
after to-morrow. And don't lose that photograph," I
added as he was leaving.

It took me all day to unload our cargo by the twisted
wreckage of the ironworks that the Germans had destroyed two years before. The burnt-brown hills that
encircle Pozzuoli shimmered in the heat and the peak of
Mt. Epomeo on the island of Ischia was barely visible in
the flaming heat haze. We got the loaded trucks off
easily enough, but when they returned from delivering
the cigarettes to a warehouse in Naples, we had to reload
them with the spares.

We only got back to our berth in Naples just in time
to change and take a taxi out to Posillipo. Stuart, who
had been morosely silent all day, did not speak during
the run out to the northern tip of the bay. But as the
driver swung in through a crest-encrusted gateway, he
suddenly said, " If the set-up here is phoney, we have
nothing to do with it—agreed ? "

I agreed.

That it was phoney, in his sense of the word, was
apparent the moment we entered the villa. The building
itself was old and it had been added to and parts of it
rebuilt at various times. It stood on rock and on the
Naples side of it was the old Palazzo Don Anna with its
archways planted firmly in the sea. The old mellow
exterior of the villa was wiped from my mind as soon as
we got inside by the welter of gilt and cupid-covered
murals. The floors were thickly carpeted and exotic
flowers were banked up against the walls, giving the place
a strange hot-house smell.

Guidici came forward to meet us and introduced us to our host, a tall, rather saturnine man with extravagant gestures and black hair, sleekly oiled. As I shook his hand I found myself looking into a pair of shrewd black eyes set close together in a lined and rather leathery face. He was somewhere between forty and fifty years old and clearly understood the world in which he lived and the people in it. His name was Guido Del Ricci.

We were shown into a long room with huge crystal chandeliers already blazing with light. At each end there were big gilt-framed mirrors. The ceiling was thick with gilt and cupids. In one corner was a big buffet table loaded with food and drinks and presided over by a white-coated servant. In the opposite corner, on a table piled high with flowers was a picture that looked suspiciously like a Titian. The room was crowded with some twenty or thirty people. The men wore lounge suits, but the women were in evening dress, some of them loaded down with jewellery which glittered in the light.

I thought of the places I had seen the previous night and I whispered to Stuart, " This is the other Italy."

He nodded. " This was the Italy of the Fascisti," he muttered. " I'd like to introduce one of the partigiani to this set-up—a grenade in places like this would do Italy a lot of good."

Our conversation was interrupted by our introduction to the assembled gathering. The frightful ceremony of shaking everybody by the hand had to be gone through. By the end of it we were none the wiser as to who we had been introduced to, but we had been left standing with two very attractive and expensively dressed girls and a maid appeared with drinks on a great silver tray. The girls stuck by us and I got the impression that they had been detailed to entertain us.

The girl who had attached herself to me said her name was Angelica. She was not exactly an angel. She had a fine full-curved body which her black and silver dress was not designed to hide. Her face was hard with full heavily made-up lips, a slightly turned-up nose, and dark smouldering eyes that gazed up at me as though I was the first man she'd ever seen. She spoke a little English—enough at any rate to tell me that my features were like those of Cesare Borgia and to suggest that we go and dance.

Three big glass doors gave on to a wide tiled terrace lit by coloured lamps. She took my arm and together we leaned over the balustrade and looked down at the dark surface of the sea. To our left the lights of Naples blazed out brazenly. A small band in a corner of the terrace began to play *Sorrento* and we danced, her body pressed close to mine. The hardness of her face melted in the soft light and the warmth of the night. Her èyes were mischievous, passionate, laughter-filled—they were pools reflecting the rhythm of the band.

The wine and her body so close to mine beat through my blood as we swayed back and forth to the pulsing of the music. Her feet were fairy light and she made love to me with her eyes and her body as we danced and danced.

And then Del Ricci broke the spell. " You will pardon me if I interrupt you, Mr. Cunningham," he said. " But I would like to talk business with you for a moment." Stuart was with him, and I saw by his eyes that he was in a black mood.

Del Ricci showed us into a quietly furnished study. " She is a nice girl, Angelica," he said, as he held the door open for me. " She is of the corps de ballet at the San Carlo Opera House. She will do well—she is a good dancer and very sympathetic."

" Cut the suave stuff, Del Ricci," Stuart said, as the door was closed. " What's your business ? "

The Italian shot him a quick glance from beneath his heavy eyelids. " I am sorry," he said, " I should have given you Julia, not Anna. She is colder and has more finesse." He went over to a decanter and poured out three large whiskies. " And now, Mr. McCrae," he said, as he handed us our glasses, " let us ignore the trimmings and get down to the basis of life—money. How much do you want for your ship ? " His eyes darted from one to the other of us as though he would read our reactions in our faces. " How much, gentlemen ? " he asked.

" Why do you think we are prepared to sell ? " asked Stuart.

" A ship is a capital asset, not a pet," was his reply. " And the value of capital assets can always be assessed."

" Why do you want to buy ? " Stuart demanded.

" Why ? " He shrugged his shoulders. " That is surely not your concern. However, I will tell you. I need her for the coastal trade. As you know Italy is very short of transport. I am interested in a big transport company. With your ship I could handle coastal trade with many little towns that even small schooners cannot supply. I hope eventually to buy several of these boats and build up a big coastal trade, which is what Italy should have."

" The possibility of building up a coastal trade has not entirely escaped us," Stuart told him. " In fact within a year, we expect to have a regular service of at least four landing craft using the West Coast."

Del Ricci smiled. " I could make it very difficult for you," he said. " Whereas if you would sell me the one boat that you have you would immediately make a very good profit which could be invested in something—a little less speculative shall we say ? " He suddenly leaned forward across his desk. " I'll give you twice what she cost new. I'll give you £20,000. I think I am mad to do it, but I need the ship to keep my transport business going. What do you say, Mr. Cunningham ? Is that a fair price ? "

" In sterling or lire ? " I asked.

" Sterling," he said.

" It's certainly a generous offer," I said. I was thinking of a clear profit of nearly £7000 each apart from the wad of lire we had banked the previous day.

Then Stuart's quiet voice cut across my thoughts. " It's certainly generous, Mr. Del Ricci," he said. " So generous, in fact, that I know very well that you are not wanting it for your normal trade."

" Naturally I should concentrate on cargoes that were urgently required."

" Arms for instance ? " Stuart's voice was harsh now.

" Now really, Mr. McCrae . . ."

Stuart took a pace forward. " Listen, Del Ricci, there was a man came to see me in London. He didn't want to buy the boat, he just wanted me to run the arms for him. I beat him up and then I threw him down a flight of stairs. Did you know that ? "

" How should I ? " His voice was steady, his features immobile. His eyes were watching Stuart. " I need your boat for trade, and I am willing to pay a high price for it."

" You are not interested in arms ? " Stuart was tapping a cigarette on the back of a silver case.

" Certainly not. Why should I be ? "

" That is what I am wondering." Stuart lit his cigarette and the match-flame lit up his bearded features and showed his eyes fixed on Del Ricci. " At my own request Julia introduced me to a certain Luigi Perroni who is here to-night."

" He is the captain of the *Pampas*. The *Pampas* is a schooner belonging to my transport company. Why ? "

" A week ago his ship was off Portugal without lights and he was talking Spanish and not Italian."

" Is that a criminal offence ? "

" No, but running arms is. And that is what he was doing. He was waiting to pick up a consignment of American munitions that had been routed via Portugal."

" That is a very grave charge, Mr. McCrae."

" I'm glad you realise the gravity of it," replied Stuart coldly.

" And it is a charge that I do not think you should make behind Perroni's back. I will get him."

" Just a moment, Del Ricci. I do not think I want to listen to Perroni's lies. I am much more interested in knowing how you stand in the matter. I have no proof that he is running arms—yet. I just know that he is, and he is running them in one of your ships. You want to buy the *Trevedra*. You have offered twice the market value and you are prepared to pay in sterling. A flat-bottomed landing craft would be a most serviceable ship for running arms. You would be able to run them ashore at any lonely beach—straight ashore in lorries as we ran our cargo this morning."

"You are levelling your accusations at me now, McCrae," Del Ricci's voice was still steady but the tone was pitched a shade higher. "That is foolish. This country is no longer run by Britain and America. It is run by us and I am a man of some standing here."

"So are some of the Black Market profiteers."

"Are you suggesting——."

"That you are a Black Market profiteer ?" Stuart shrugged his shoulders. "I know that you have a reputation as a clever business man, that your transport company controls all road transport in certain districts and that in those districts essential foodstuffs sold by another concern in which you are interested, the South Italy Produce Coy, are considerably more expensive than in other districts. Arms can be very useful to those who are exploiting the people to the point of desperation."

"I think you must be mad to make accusations like this." Del Ricci's eyes were brightly watchful and a nerve at the side of his forehead pulsed tensely.

"Mad ! " Stuart's eyes blazed suddenly and the last vestige of liquor-warmth seeped out of me as I sensed the tension in the atmosphere. "I lost most of my best friends in this bloody country because a band of hooligans in black shirts marched on Rome some twenty-five years ago. Where did they get their arms ? They took control of the country for men of standing who gave them the money to do it and who, in exchange, had exploitation legalised and made it the biggest national industry.

"Go up the roads to Cassino and Pescara, by Pisa and Florence and through the hills to Rimini. Do you know

what those rows and rows of white crosses mean?
Everyone of them represents the body of a boy killed
in the prime of his life because it paid somebody to
give a bunch of hooligans arms in 1922. Do you think
I am mad to want to see that that does not happen
again?"

"If you are so sure of yourself, why don't you go to
the Questura?" There was no mistaking the sneer in
Del Ricci's voice.

"What—in your own territory? A hell of a lot of
good that would do. You've already threatened me.
You've already said, 'I can make it difficult for you.'
That threat was not made lightly. You know your own
power."

"And you know yours apparently."

"What do you mean?" Stuart's body was tensed—
the whole room was electric. I was very conscious of the
fact that we were foreigners in a foreign land.

Del Ricci chuckled and the sound was false in that
silent room. "When you had the Americans and the
Poles and the Indians and the Greeks fighting for you,
you didn't worry about the rights of the Italians to run
their own country. But now——"

Stuart crossed the room very slowly and Del Ricci's
words ceased as he saw him approach. He seemed
fascinated. "Do you know how many British boys
died or were wounded in Italy to free this country
from Fascism? They died in their thousands—and all
because they believed in the freedom of peoples to
govern their own countries. They were just workers and
farm labourers, bank clerks and shopkeepers—and they
died that their own country, and all the other countries
of the world, should be free." Stuart was towering above
Del Ricci. Del Ricci slipped his hand inside his jacket.
He was frightened. It was then that Stuart hit him. He
hit him between the eyes. And Del Ricci was flung back
against a bookcase, his head smashing in the glass, and
then his body slowly crumpled, his head bleeding pro-
fusely from a cut.

Stuart bent down, slipped his hand inside Del Ricci's jacket and removed a small revolver from an armpit holster. " Come on," he said. " Let's get out of here." He opened the door and the silence of the room was invaded by the sound of the band playing *Funicoli, Funicola* amid the murmur of voices and the chink of glass.

Outside, the city was bright in moonlight. The façades of the villas and apartment houses climbing the hill to the Vomero district were white and full of light and beyond Capri the low-hung disc of the moon shone a path of silver across the dark mirror of the sea.

" That wasn't very wise, was it ? " I said.

He made no reply. He was taking long strides and I had difficulty in keeping up with him.

" And what proof had you that he was running arms ? You can't just accuse——"

He stopped suddenly. " For Christ sake, shut up," he said. His eyes glared down at me. He was all tensed up. " If you're prepared to deal with a dirty little Sicilian crook who is making a pile out of his country's misfortunes, go ahead. But count me out."

" Don't be absurd, Stuart," I said. " I wasn't suggesting you deal with him. I was——"

" I know what you were suggesting," he rapped out, and his teeth were clenched. He was fighting for control of himself. " You were suggesting that I should have been more polite, that I shouldn't have hit him when he went for his gun. You people make me sick. You'd see the whole wretched business start all over again. You'd try to persuade yourself that all the crooks grafting their way to power are innocent until proved guilty. And in the end you'll shrug your shoulders and say that war is inevitable as you watch another million British war graves planted on the Continent."

" That's ridiculous," I said. " All I am——"

" All right—I'm a fool. I should forget." He gripped my shoulders and the edge of his nail bit through the cloth of my jacket. " But I can't forget," he said. " I can't forget. Do you understand what that means? I can't forget that I've seen boys who should have been taking girls out, shrieking hideously and holding their guts with their hands, that pieces of flesh have been spattered all over me, and that I've watched a company of brave men die one by one. And the bodies of the partigiani horribly mutilated up in the Chianti country. And I can't forget that my wife and kid were burned to death. And it all started here in this country when a bunch of crooks got control and went berserk. God!" He turned abruptly and started walking again.

Back on the *Trevedra*, Stuart made tea. He was quite calm again as we sat in the wardroom drinking and smoking, and he told me what he had found out about Del Ricci. "As soon as I talked to Perroni I knew what Del Ricci's proposition was going to be. Perroni knew what it was, too. I fancy he was going to get command of the ship if we'd sold. Then I talked to a man who was a director on the board of Del Ricci's transport company. He spoke a little English, and reading between the lines I got an impression of the whole set-up. It's based on monopoly, of course. Individuals and small private concerns who attempt to compete don't do so well. One big concern had tried to muscle in, but a series of unfortunate fires had cramped their style and they'd had to sell out. He told me that with a dazzling smile which made it difficult to realise that it was to be taken as a threat. Del Ricci has a finger in all sorts of pies—produce, tobacco, furniture, coal—anything that needs transporting. He is also a director of the new Banco Nazionale di Riconstruzione. And, most significant of all, he is one of the interests behind the Massa del Popolo Party which was started about three months ago with its headquarters here in Naples.

"Well," he concluded, "that's Mr. Del Ricci for you. And he's done all that in less than two years. Clearly a bloke to be reckoned with. I should have been more careful perhaps, but——" he shrugged his shoulders.

" I got mad, that was all. If you like to take your share of the proceeds and get out I shan't blame you."

" No," I said. " This is my life now. All I would suggest is that in future we talk things over before acting. I agree with your view of Del Ricci, but beating him up doesn't get us anywhere."

He nodded gloomily. " I should have shot him," he said, and then he began to laugh.

CHAPTER SIX

THE TRAIL ENDS IN TUSCANY

At three o'clock the next day I met Pietro in the Galleria. He had traced the Gallianis up to a point. Their flat in the Via Santa Cecilia was no longer there. It had been in a big block just behind the Metropole on the sea front. The whole block had been destroyed in one of the big raids before the Salerno landing.

"But I find their cook," Pietro said. "I speak her about them and she say they are in the ricovero and not kilt." I told him to speak Italian. I was in no mood to have him try his English out on me.

They had apparently moved into rooms in the Vico Tiratoio, one of the squalid little streets on the north side of the Via Roma. Pietro had got the address and had seen the owner of the place just before meeting me. From his description of it, Galliani must have been in a pretty bad way financially. The entrance was up a dark staircase next to a *trattoria* that sold cheap vino from Ischia. On the first floor had been a tailor's shop, the Galliani's had had the second, the third floor had belonged to a journalist on *Il Mattino* and the top floor had been a *bordello*.

"The girl was with them ? " I asked.

He nodded. "*Si, signore*, the girl was with them. They were there three months."

"And then ? "

"They could not pay so they went to the farm of his cousin which is at Itri."

"What was the name of the cousin ? " I asked.

"This is the address." He handed me a slip of paper. On it was written, "Furigo Ciprio, Santa Brigida, Itri."

From where I sat I looked down the finely-paved expanse of the Galleria across the traffic of the Via Roma to the narrow entrance of a street of tall, dirty buildings, that

ran straight up the hill to the Corso Vittorio Emanuele.
In one of those streets up there Mrs. Dupont's daughter
had lived for three months. It wasn't difficult to picture
the circumstances of this family as Pietro told me the
gossip he had gleaned. Galliani had been a dapper little
man, the manager of a small shipping firm. The business
had died. A shop that he acquired as a side-line had
been looted during the raid in which he had lost his flat.
When he came to the Vico Tiratoio he had begun to
drink. But he clung to Naples because he thought he
could get a job. His wife took in washing and the girl,
besides helping with this, did embroidery work. Three
months of that and then they had given up and gone to
his cousin's farm.

I thanked Pietro for his help. " I'll go up to the farm
to-morrow," I said. " Will you arrange for a car to pick
me up at the docks at nine o'clock." I paid him off then.

I wandered slowly down the Galleria with its café
tables full of dark-haired girls and men in open-necked
shirts and suits of fantastically brilliant colours. It was
very hot and the Via Roma thrust itself upon me with a
dull roar of traffic. I crossed the hot soft-tarred thorough-
fare and forced my way through the crowds into the Via
Buoncompagni.

The tall houses closed in on me—cool, quiet and
squalid. The sound of traffic was dulled and its place
taken by individual sounds of children's voices and people
calling to each other. The streets were cleaner than when
I had last seen them. The squatters from the bombed-
out areas of the docks were gone. There was no sign of
garbage or outdoor cooking on improvised wood or char-
coal fires. New shops were open and some of the houses
had been repainted. I noticed these things automatically
for my mind was engrossed in the picture of the life of a
half-English, half-French girl in an Italian family who
were in difficulties at the time when the Germans still
occupied Naples.

I found the house without difficulty. It was No. 29,
just on the corner where the Vico Tiratoio meets the Via

Sergente Maggiore. It was just as Pietro had described it. There was the little *trattoria*. The sour smell of vino seeped out into the street. As I stood there the bead curtains parted and a seaman staggered out. He stood for a moment blinking in the sunlight and swaying slightly back on to his heels. He gazed round and then lurched into the doorway next to the *trattoria*. His boots sounded hesitantly as he climbed the dark, bare-boarded stairs that Monique must have used. Over the entrance-way was a gaudily-painted image of the Virgin set in a weather-worn wooden frame with two tinsel-covered electric light bulbs and a posy of artificial white flowers. I took out the photograph of Monique that Pietro had returned to me. The innocence of the girl in that faded picture was appalling when considered against the background of her life. I was determined to find out what had happened to her.

I told Stuart this when I got back to the ship and he was quite agreeable. He said it would take him two more days to complete the purchase of our cargo. I arranged to take Boyd with me for company.

Itri is a little town beyond the Garigliano on the coast road from Naples to Rome. This road is Highway Seven, the route the American Fifth Army took. We came down to it by way of Caserta. Boyd wanted to see the palace, not because it was the second largest and quite the ugliest in Europe, but because he wanted to take " a decco at the Bras 'Ats' Palis "—it had been the Head-quarters of the Allied Armies in Italy all through the bitter fighting of the winter of 1943-44. The great square red-brick structure, with the railway line which had been built to pass within a hundred yards of the windows for the amusement of the Royal Family, looked useless. The gardens were still as unkempt as they had been when they were a park for Army trucks. Only the long artificial lake, where Field-Marshall Alexander had kept his own wizzer seaplanes, seemed pleasant, and that was violently unreal against the natural setting of the hills.

Beyond Capua we forked left, away from Highway

D.A.

Six, the road to Cassino. We had crossed the Volturno
by a Bailey bridge that had been built by our own engineers
to replace the blown Roman bridge. It was the same at
the Gariglino. The temporary Bailey structure still
spanned the road that crossed the river. " *Sono bravi
ingegneri, gli Inglesi,*" was our driver's comment. At
Formia the buildings shattered by the naval bombard-
ment had been cleared so that there was a good view of
Gaeta across the blue of the bay. But the town was still
bedraggled with the marks of war in the side streets.
All sorts of temporary buildings had been erected on the
shattered foundations of the original houses. And Itri,
set on a hill beneath the sprawling bulk of the Monti
Aurunci, was even worse. It was a little town of flies and
dust and rubble pulsing lazily in the midday heat. At
the post office they told us how to find the farm. " But
Signor Furigo does not live there now," they said. It
was burned and he was killed. Of the Galliani's they knew
nothing.

" This is getting to be like a bleedin' treasure hunt,"
Boyd said as we got into the car again.

The farm was at the end of a dusty track. The wreck
of a burned-out building stood among the olive trees and
the ground shimmered in the sun's heat trapped in the
bowl of the hills. The remains of a barn had been made
into a shack and nearby on a patch of brick-hard earth
two women with kerchiefs tied around their heads were
beating at a pile of wheat stalks. They were threshing in
the old way. It was from them that I learned what had
happened when the Germans were in Itri and the Fifth
Army was across the river where the bridge had been
blown.

It had been late in May. A German 88 mm. battery had
established itself among the olive groves of Santa Brigida.
They were tired and desperate. The Garigliano had been
crossed by the Americans little more than a week ago
and there were reports of rapid progress by the Eighth
beyond Cassino. They had lost two guns and over thirty
men. The Commandant ordered Furigo to hand over all

livestock, wine and grain. He took over the farmhouse as his headquarters. The barn and outhouses were occupied by his men. Furigo and his wife with their two daughters, the Gallianis with the "French" girl and these two women who were born in Itri and had worked on the farm since their husbands had been killed in the desert, were forced to sleep in the open.

The Germans fired their 88's steadily until the following afternoon in an attempt to stem the crossing of the fosse. The two women described the scene volubly with many gesticulations. Repeatedly they pointed to the ruined bulk of Itri, the thick fortress walls of which towered above the valley farm, cracked and broken.

It had been blasted by bombers and ground to rubble by the artillery. From the shelter of a stone wall they had watched their little town gradually disintegrate and wilt away in great spouting billows of dust and debris. Then the roar of the guns had slackened and the chatter of machine guns and thud of mortars had taken up the symphony of death. The German battery brought their guns out of action, hitched up and began to move off. But before they went two soldiers began to throw petrol on to the straw in the barn and on to the door posts of the outhouses, and even the farmhouse itself. They set fire to the barn first and then one by one the outhouses.

But when they went to the house Furigo, who had built it with his own hands, rushed up to them, pleading. Galliani was with him. The soldiers thrust him aside and went to the little wooden porch of the house, one carrying a tin of petrol and the other a torch made of petrol-soaked rag tied to the end of a stick.

As the soldier with the can splashed the petrol on to the wood of the porch Furigo seized his arm. He was crying, pleading, on his knees. The soldier brought his boot up sharply, catching the farmer on the chin. And as he fell back he tipped the rest of the petrol on to him. Without hesitation the other thrust the flaming brand against the wretched man's clothing. Furigo rose with a terrible shriek—he was a sheet of flame. The women said that for a moment they saw him, running, lit up by the flames, his eyes wide, his mouth open, shrieking terribly. Then his flesh had blackened and suddenly he had seemed to shrivel and collapse.

At the same time a shot rang out. Galliani, who had been struggling to prevent the soldier from setting fire to the wretched man, staggered and fell with blood oozing from a throat wound. Furigo's wife, who had followed her husband, watched him burn alive and then with a shriek turned on the Germans and attacked them with her bare hands. They shot her too—in the face. Then they threw her body and Galliani's into the porch and set light to it.

" The smell of burned flesh was in the valley for days," one of the women said. Her eyes were dilated. She was re-living the ghastly scene as she told it to us.

" And Signora Galliani and the girl ? " I asked.

There had been no work, no food but what they could beg from the Americans passing through. The Signora knew of a man who owned a farm at Pericele up in the Abruzzi to the east of Rome. Early in July she and the girl had left Itri, walking north along the dusty road towards Rome.

I looked round the olive groves, so serene and quiet in the hot sun. It seemed incredible that these silvery-leaved trees had once been dumb witnesses to the horrible scene that these two women had described. I thanked them and gave them some money, and we went back down the track leaving a swirling cloud of dust rolling in our tyre tracks.

" Pericele ? " Boyd asked as we reached the road.

I nodded.

The driver turned left and we went down the valley to Fondi and Terracina. Round the towering quarry-scarred headland we launched out on the arrow-straight road that runs through the Pontine Marshes to the Alban Hills and the Appian Way into Rome. We stopped once near Terracina to get the dust out of our throats with *cocomero*, the red country melon of Italy that is full of pips and water, and again at Genzano where we had good *vino bianco* in a little *trattoria* perched high above a small lake clutched in the bowl of what had once been a crater.

The map which we had brought with us showed Pericele to the east of Tivoli. " We'd better stay the night in Rome," I suggested to Boyd.

The Eternal City seemed strange without the mass of khaki that had filled its wide pavements to overflowing when last I had seen it. We came into the city by way of the Colosseum and that monstrous wedding cake of a monument that dominates the Piazza Venezia. The Via del Tritone, once the Broadway of Rome with more GI pick-ups to its credit than Shaftesbury Avenue before D-Day, looked comparatively deserted. There were fewer bicycles and fewer tarts.

I went straight to the Hotel de la Ville where I had stayed a night when it was crowded with British and American war correspondents just after the Fifth Army had entered the city. The Fascist name, Albergo Citta, had been dropped.

After booking a room on the seventh floor with a terrace, I fixed Boyd and the Italian driver up at a Swiss *pensione* opposite. Back in my room I was suddenly conscious of a sense of loneliness. I went out on to the terrace and looked across the mellow brickwork of the ancient city to the great crouching bulk of St. Peter's dome beyond the Tiber. Back in the dim past of the war I had stood on one of these terraces and looked across to the Gianicolo, and I had the same feeling now as then— of a city that was outside the reality of life.

Rome is a city, founded on religion, that has degenerated to a point where its people pay lip-service only to its five hundred churches and to the great sprawling palaces of the Vatican, living a life of pleasure in which any sense of responsibility to the world at large is totally lacking. That was what the war correspondents had told me that first night in the hotel bar. Whilst the guns were thundering at Trasimene and there was starvation in the refugee-crowded back streets, Rome society had talked mostly of parties and how nice it had been the year before when they could go out in their cars to villas at Frascati and Tivoli and Ostia for the hot summer months.

A girl came out on to the terrace of the neighbouring room and shot me a quick glance beneath a mop of dark hair. She wore a white evening gown cut low to disclose the swell of full sun-tanned breasts. She leaned upon the balustrade and looked down on to the roof garden across the street where people were sitting at ease in the evening sun watching two children playing hide-and-seek with shrill voices in and out of the green shrubs.

A thick-set man with an almost bald head came out and joined her on the terrace. They held hands for a minute or two looking out across the warm bricks of the ancient city to that monstrosity of white marble in the Piazza Venezia that looks more like a monument to the fallen pretensions of fascism than a memorial to the dead of the first World War. Then they went back into their room.

That is Rome—old men, rich in corruption, and smart attractive women with no souls, offering their bodies in fee for security with side-kicks on the quiet for pleasure.

I turned back into my room, the sense of loneliness strong in me. It was a feeling that not even the exotic warmth of a bath could dispel. But as I lay relaxed in the soapy water with the sunlight slanting in through the open french windows, I understood the reason for it. For three months now I had been married to a ship. For three months I had been fully occupied, mentally and physically. I had been living with men who were alive and interested in doing a job. Now I was alone for the first time since my arrival at Trevedra—and I was alone in this pleasure city where people went to bed together too often and loved too seldom. When I had been here before the essential rottenness of its way of life had been half-hidden beneath the purposeful khaki figures of men who knew where they were going and intended to get there. Now Rome had been handed back to the Romans. The little men with bad teeth and a penchant for fish and chips and their big slouching, gum-chewing, hunker-squatting allies were gone. And I was in civvies instead of a naval uniform.

The sense of loneliness was inevitable.

Dinner was in the tiled courtyard on the second floor. I had a table to myself and a bottle of Spumante. And then I strolled up to the gardens of the Villa Borghese and watched the sun set behind the dome of St Peter's in a gold and purple sky.

Back in my room at the hotel the first thing I noticed was the faded photograph of Monique Dupont lying on the table by my bed. I could not remember taking it out of my suitcase. But there it was—the picture of a girl of fifteen. Now she would be twenty-two, and if all went well I should meet her to-morrow.

I lay awake till the moonlight flooded the room and the tiles of Rome gleamed white between the bars of the balustrade—thinking about the girl. Though it was more than a month ago that I had read it, her mother's letter was still fresh in my mind. I had read it on the sands of Plymouth Sound. Now I was in Rome on my way to meet this girl whom I only knew through an old and faded photograph. It was a strange quest. But now that I had undertaken it and come so far in my search it had become almost a personal thing.

Just over two years ago she had been working on a farm in Itri. She had then travelled to a place near Rome after the fall of the city. Presuming that she was an attractive girl, what would be the effect of a nature half English, half French, exiled in war-torn Italy for six years ? Clearly she would have seen more of life than most girls of her own class at that age. She had been in Naples during the bombing. She had lived in the disease-ridden, garbage-cluttered streets beyond the Via Roma for three months. She had worked as a farm girl and seen the farm and its owners destroyed by the Germans. She had trekked north to another farm.

If she were still at that farm, she would have been there for over two years. Allowing that she was a normal, passionate girl, with as much of the animal as there should be in a human being, what would have become of her ? Would she have married a local farmer's boy ? Or would she still be with her aunt, a young woman working on a farm with half the village lads sniffing round the house ? Or—far more likely—would I have to seek her in Rome itself, a typist, the wife of some shopkeeper or the mistress of a business man ?

In view of the thoughts that kept me awake so long, it is not surprising that I started out for Pericele in the morning with a sense of excitement not unmixed with foreboding.

The sulphur springs on the way to Tivoli were open. And in Tivoli itself there were tourist buses in the square outside the Villa d'Este, the great house where the Borgias once lived. One wing had been destroyed by bombs. The rest remained, a monument to man's fascination for the sound of falling water. The gardens of the villa fall steeply to the gorge that contains the water of the falls and every path ends in a fountain or is arched with water.

We took the Arsoli road east as far as Vicovaro, and then turned left up into the hills past the Villa d'Orazio, where the poet Horace wrote his odes, sublimely oblivious over his rich red Tuscan wine that they would become the bane of children studying the classics through the ages.

Pericele was another of these mountain villages perched precariously on top of a hill. It was almost like being back in Sicily, for a naval officer does not get far inland and this was my first sight of the Abruzzi Mountains. We were already more than 2,000 feet up. All around us were peaks rising to 5,000 feet. They hemmed us in, so that there was no air and it was hotter than it was down in the *campagna*.

We passed the rusting remains of a burnt-out tank and the brown twisted carcases of two lorries that had clearly been stripped by the local inhabitants of all useful parts in the same way that vultures strip the flesh from a dead animal. The grass was still lush here in the valley. The road ended abruptly at a blown bridge that had still not been repaired and we dipped sharply to the bed of the stream on a diversion that had originally been bull-dozed by Eighth Army engineers. The broken arches of the bridge that had once spanned the fosse strode across the floor of the little valley like petrified giants raising their gaunt mortar arms to heaven in impotent fury.

Though time had weathered the destructive effect of high explosive, it was still clear that for a brief moment war had filled this little valley, now lying lazy and pleasant in the heat, with the thunder of guns and bombs and the chatter of small arms fire. There were bullet scars on the stone work of the viaduct and the roof of the little church on the other side of the stream showed the brighter colouring of new tiles as though they were battle scars.

Beside the empty stream ran a small stone aqueduct. And though it was the dry season, it was still feeding water into big concrete storage tanks. These tanks held the water that kept the grinding wheels of a mill half-hidden among the trees at the end of a short track turning all the year round.

And high above the valley and the little church and the broken arches and the mill towered the village of Pericele. The windows of its houses looked out above our heads to the mountains and there was no sign of life.

A bullock cart was coming down the track on the other side of the ford. A woman walked beside two great lumbering beasts. A man, walking up the track, shouted and waved a short cane. He quickened his pace. The bullocks stopped. The woman cringed away from him as he approached the stationary cart. He towered above her, a big man in riding breeches and gaiters. He pointed to the yoke. The cane flashed twice in the sun. The girl flung her arms up, her back against the side of the cart.

And then the scene was suddenly normal again. The bullocks were plodding on down the track. The woman was walking beside the cart, having adjusted the yoke. And the man with the cane was walking on up the track to the main road. As we splashed through the ford I was wondering whether he had really struck her or whether I had just day-dreamed it.

The bullock cart pulled in to let us pass. It was piled with dung and the flies buzzed incessantly. The driver was not a woman—it was a girl. She was tall and fair-haired, which is unusual in the peasants of the Tuscan hills. Her face was pale and strained. It was not beautiful, but it had a quality that made me look at her closely. She wore a plain black dress. It hung on her loosely, for it had no belt. Her feet were bare and grey with dust, her hair hung damply on her head. But she had a certain pride of body—her breasts thrust tautly at the sack-like dress and she walked erect and easily. Her eyes met mine as we drove slowly past the cart. They were grey unhappy eyes.

We rejoined the interrupted road and turned up the hill to Pericele. I looked closely at the man with the cane as we passed. He was big and thick-set with heavy brutal features. Somehow he seemed to fit the primitive surroundings. He walked with the air of a man who was cock of his own particular walk. He was like a prize bull—a powerful animal of a man with a passionate nature and a hasty temper. I felt sorry for the girl with the grey eyes. Clearly he regarded her as a serf.

But I didn't stop. To explain to a man that women should not be beaten to ensure that they do what they are told was clearly a waste of time up here in the hills— and dangerous. The law does not mean all that much up in the mountain villages where the feudal system still exists in fact, though not in theory.

Dark stone houses, buzzing with flies, closed in on us as we climbed the road to the village. Faces appeared as though by magic at every window. And women, fat and

THE TRAIL ENDS IN TUSCANY 91

slovenly and work-worn, crowded to their doorways to see us pass, a thousand brats clinging to their black dirt-stained skirts. Young girls, olive-skinned, dark-eyed and sexually uninhibited, smiled and giggled at us as we went by.

Clearly our arrival was an event in the village.

We reached a little square with the inevitable fountain in the centre. Here old men sat smoking in the sun and women were doing the washing in the cold mountain water. The first tomato crop had been gathered in and on every ledge and roof and even in the street in front of the houses the red fruit, halved, lay drying in the sun, the pips showing yellow. We stopped and children crowded around the car. They did not speak. They just stared, wide-eyed.

I asked for the village priest, and we were directed across the square to a narrow little street that was barely wide enough for the car. It had once been stepped. But the stones were worn and time and the villagers had filled it with so much dirt that it was possible to use it as a road.

The sound of the old Lancia as it stormed the hill was shatteringly loud. The road was so narrow that we seemed to be thrusting the grey houses and the crowding faces of the villagers back on either side. Children ran behind us, clinging to the bumpers and the spare wheel.

So we reached the very summit of the village. And here, in a little square, was the priest's house. It was not really a square. It was just that the road widened out where it stopped at a grey stone wall. There were houses on one side. But on the other, a wall topped with drying tomatoes guarded a sheer drop to the valley floor. We stopped the car and found ourselves looking down upon the road by which we had come, all flanked by mountains, towards Rome and the sea.

"Blimey!" said Boyd, as he got out and saw the silent gaping crowd of children, "we might be the Pied Piper like."

The word " Inglese " was whispered through the clutter
of small faces. A ragged urchin with dark eager eyes
came up to Boyd and said, " *Sigaretta, Johnnie ?* " The
old cries burst forth then in a clamour of small voices.
" *Cioccolata ! Sigaretta ! Hey, Johnnie, gomma !* "

" *Silenzio !* "

The babel of voices froze. The door of one of the houses
had opened and a dark-haired man with a thin face and
deep-socketed eyes stood in the doorway, his hands
white against the folds of his black gown.

His dark eyes stared at me unwinking as I told him
who I was looking for. Not a muscle of his face moved,
but at the name Galliani I had a feeling of tension.

" Galliani ! " he said. " Maria Galliani. She worked
for Guido Mancini down in the valley. She is dead now."
He said it with a disinterested bluntness that was either
callousness or the familiarity with death that is perhaps
inevitable in a man of his profession.

" When did she die ? " I asked.

" Just over a year ago. It must have been shortly
after she came to the village. She had suffered and it was
too much for her."

" And what about the girl ? "

" The girl," he repeated. And I had the impression
he was playing for time. Or perhaps it was my imagination. There seemed no vestige of humanity in him. His
voice was cold, unhelpful, as though he resented being
questioned about a member of his flock.

" The French girl," I said. " Her name was Monique
Dupont."

" I know of no girl of that name in the village."

" But surely," I said, " Signora Galliani brought with
her a girl when she came to live in the village. She would
have been about twenty."

He seemed to hesitate. Then he said, " Ah yes, it is
possible that she has some French blood. She is fair—
not like our mountain people. She was Maria Galliani's
niece. Her name is Monica. Why are you interested ? "

I told him then about Monique's mother in England

and how I had followed the trail of the girl from Naples to Itri and on to Pericele.

He said nothing when I had finished. He stood there quite silent for a moment. He might have been praying for guidance. Or he might have been thinking out his line of action. At any rate he suddenly said, " *Scusate* " and disappeared into the house.

CHAPTER SEVEN

THE FRENCH GIRL

WHEN the priest came out again he had on his wide-brimmed black hat. His quick scurrying walk, which scattered the children out of his path, made him look like a black beetle hurrying about its urgent affairs. " I will take you to see the grave of Maria Galliani," he said and bustled into the car. As we moved back down the hill to the village square he said, " Are you a Catholic ? "

I shook my head.

His white hands fluttered in an expression of resignation. " I was thinking that you might have liked to give a candle for her. The English are always so generous." He shot me a quick glance and then sighed. " The little church where she is buried is very poor and much repair work had to be done after the battle by the bridge. But God was merciful. He damaged only His own house and left the village untouched."

He directed the driver down through the village to the ford and the little church in the valley. We were met at the door by an old man with a grey beard and watery eyes. The priest motioned Boyd and myself inside.

Like everything about the village the church was depressingly primitive. It was cool and almost damp inside and the peeling walls were festooned with tawdry gilt and white plaques to the dead of the village. On the wall opposite the door a life-size figure of Christ hung dejectedly from its cross. It was badly carved in wood and on a shelf at its feet stood jam jars of faded summer flowers.

I don't think I have ever seen such an ugly interior to a church. The villagers seemed to have vied with one another to hang upon its walls the most gaudy memorials possible within their means: even to little glass or celophane cases filled with artificial lillies.

The priest had stopped by the door to talk to the old man. But now he came in and led us up to the altar. " These were carved by Maria Galliani," he said, pointing to a pair of candlesticks delicately worked in some local wood. On the base of each was carved the name of her husband—Emilio Galliani—and the sign of peace.

" In the cemetery you can see her grave," the priest said, leading us out again into the bright sunlight. " She had not worked long with Guido Mancini, but he bought her a good headstone."

By the great marble tomb of the Iori family, half-hidden by two black crosses that marked the graves of German soldiers killed in the fighting at the ford, was a sandstone boulder. On it was roughly carved—" *Hic Jacet Maria Galliani, Requiescat in Pace.*" There were wild roses in a little sunken vase.

" And now, what about the girl ? " I asked, as he showed no sign of moving.

" The girl ? Ah, yes—she is at Mancini's farm. She is all right. But she will be up in the hills now, minding the goats. It will be difficult to find her." His eyes watched me out of their dark sockets.

" Then let's go to the farm and see," I said.

He shrugged his shoulders. " If you will wait while I have a word with the wife of the man who looks after the church. She has been ill and it would be unkind if I came here and did not visit her."

I nodded, and he led us back through the cemetery and disappeared into the open doorway of the cottage attached to the church.

" Like a bloody beetle scurryin' into 'is 'ole, ain't 'e," said Boyd. " Somehow I never trusts them blokes. I seen quite a bit of 'em in the little fishing villages along the coast an' I always 'ad a feeling they was living on the igorance of the people."

It was nearly ten minutes before the priest reappeared. He got into the car and we drove on down the track, across the ford and then turned left below the broken arches of the bridge. Beyond the mill the track turned right and ran along the banks of the stream through a cool tunnel of trees. At the end of this track stood Mancini's farm.

It was a biggish place of grey stone cluttered with out-houses. The farmyard was strewn with dung that steamed in the midday heat. The lazy hum of flies was the only sound when the Lancia's engine stopped. A small boy came out of the house with a sly sidelong glance. His hands were deep thrust into the pockets of trousers that had once been khaki serge and there was milk on his upper lip which he kept on licking at with quick nervous movements of his tongue.

The priest knocked at the door and a dog barked lazily as though the effort were too much for him in the heat. The flies buzzed incessantly, settling clingingly in the sweat of face and neck. The door with its blistered paint opened suddenly and framed in the darkness of the interior of the house stood a woman of about thirty-five.

She was a big woman with wide hips and breasts that sagged unsupported beneath her black cotton dress. Her hair clung dankly to her head, which was large for a woman, and she wore a pair of big gold earings. Her lips were a thin bitter line in the olive skin of her face and she had the dark brown eyes of a bitch that has been whipped too often to expect any good to come of life. Her belly was big with child and where it stretched her dress the cotton was a deeper black with sweat. Her legs, braced wide apart to support the weight of her, were marked with bites which showed a dull red through dark hair. Her big peasant feet were thrust incon-gruously into an expensive pair of mules, the finery of which was filmed with dirt and threadbare with constant wear.

" There is an Englishman here to see the Galliani girl," the priest said.

She spread out her hands in the Italian gesture of

resignation and I saw a great purple bruise on the inside of her left arm. " The girl is in the hills looking after the goats," she said. She said it flatly, without expression, as though we ought to know that the girl was in the hills looking after the goats.

The priest shrugged his shoulders. " I am sorry," he said to me. " It is as I told you. She will not be down until the sun sets and to search for her on the hills would not be good in the heat. But at least your journey has not been wasted. You will be able to tell her mother that she is all right and well cared for. When Maria Galliani died she made Guido Mancini the girl's guardian. He is prosperous, as you see. He will find her a good match and he has agreed to provide her with a *dote*."

" Who is this woman ? " I asked. I did not like the unctuous tones of the priest's voice nor the way he took it for granted that I would not wait to see the girl.

" This is Signora Mancini."

I made no comment. I was not impressed by the woman's appearance. She looked bitter and cowed. The primitive atmosphere of the village seemed to linger here in the flaming heat of the farmyard. I told Boyd to take a look round the outhouses. Somehow I wasn't quite convinced that the girl really was away in the hills.

" Is there anything else you wish to know about the girl whilst you are here ? " the priest asked.

" I'd like to have a word with this man Mancini," I told him. I was thinking of Mrs. Dupont back in England, struggling against ill health to earn a living at a typewriter, her daughter the only thing she had left to live for. Was it enough to go back and tell her that her daughter was a goat-herd at a farm up in the Abruzzi ?

" You are thinking perhaps that it is hard for a girl who has been well brought up to be working on a farm ? " suggested the priest with uncanny insight. " But, remember, the girl is not the girl her mother knew. She has seen much poverty. And she is now accustomed to

D.A.

this life. She has no other home in Italy. And she has assumed Italian nationality."

That brought my thoughts up with a jolt. It would make it difficult for me to take her out of the country, even if I were willing to assume such a responsibility. " When was she naturalised ? " I asked.

" Just after she and her aunt settled here."

I turned away from the farm. Perhaps it would be best to leave well alone. " I would like to meet Mancini," I said.

" He is up in the village now," the priest said. " But by the time we get back he will have completed his business there and then he will go on the rounds of his farm. You may have to wait until this evening if you wish to see him."

I hesitated. That would make another day. Stuart would be wondering what the hell I was up to. As I tried to make up my mind what to do, Boyd suddenly appeared from behind one of the barns and came hurrying towards us.

" Mr. Cunningham," he called out excitedly, " you remember that bullock cart we met as we crossed the ford coming into the village this morning ? "

I nodded.

" Well, it's right here in the farm, still full of dung with all the flies in Pericele buzzing round it. But I don't see no sign of the girl."

" The girl ! "

Good God ! Of course—the girl. Fair hair and grey unhappy eyes. And the man who'd struck her—that would have been Mancini. And then I remembered the little boy who had slunk out of the farm as we drove up and the way the woman had said the girl was up in the hills in the flat-toned way people do when they've been told to say something that they know to be untrue.

I glanced at the priest. He hadn't understood what Boyd had said, but he sensed that something was wrong and his dark eyes flickered between us.

I went over to the Lancia. " When we were at the church, did a little boy speak to the old man and then come down to this farm ? " I asked the driver.

He nodded. " It was the one who was leaving the farm as we drove up."

So that was it. I swung round on the priest. " Get into the car," I said. I was seething with anger.

It was the wrong line. I knew that as soon as I had said it. I should have been more subtle. Now I had frightened him. I saw fear leap like a wounded rabbit into his eyes as they shifted from the car and me and on to Boyd. Then he jumped for the open door of the farm, flapping through the entrance like a great black crow that has had its wings clipped.

Before Boyd or I could move the door had closed. The bolts shot home with a rasping sound and we were left staring at the blistered paintwork.

" Well, of all the bleedin'——" Boyd checked the stream of obscenities that rose unconsciously to his lips. " Wot d'you reck'n his game was anyway ? " he asked.

I couldn't answer that one. But I was determined to find out.

" Here come the chuckers-out," Boyd said.

A small man with a village-made straw hat on his head had come into the farmyard. He had a shotgun under his arm. The double barrels gleamed bluely in the sun. The driver began talking fast in Italian. It was plain he was getting scared.

" I think a word with the small boy would help," I said, and the driver beamed with relief as we climbed into the car.

Back at the church we found the boy sitting on a tombstone swinging his legs and carving a boat out of a piece of wood. The mention of the word *Polizia* and the offer of a bar of chocolate had the desired effect. The priest had told him to tell Signora Mancini to send the girl to a neighbouring farm and to tell the English when they came that she was up in the hills with the goats.

" Where is the farm ? " I asked.

He pointed beyond the broken arches of the bridge back along the road to Vicovaro. For twenty lire he agreed to show us.

It was a little mud and stone building in the valley below the main road. We left the car and went down a footpath through a field of bare sticks where tomato plants had already yielded their crop and on through a field of ripening maize that was a warm yellow in the sunlight. A donkey stared at us disinterestedly and a few hens picked in the dirt around the one door. A mangy cat was asleep on the stone doorstep. The sound of running water from the stream mingled with the low hum of flies.

We knocked on the door. But not even a dog barked. The place seemed lifeless in the heat. We went on round the back where a dirt track wound along the banks of the stream to the Mancini farm just visible in its screen of trees about a kilometre away.

A rough vegetable patch sloped to the tree-lined banks of the stream. The sound of water was now mingled with the shriller sound of women's voices. We continued down the dusty path until we could see the yellow pebble bed of the stream. A grey-haired peasant woman was kneeling down on an outcrop of shingle rubbing at clothes in the thin trickle of the stream.

Near her was the girl we had seen with the bullock cart. Her fair hair was tumbled over her eyes and she was washing the grey film of dirt off her feet. She had the drab skirt of her dress drawn up to her thighs and her limbs were whiter than those of any Italian girl I had seen.

She was laughing at a small sheep-dog that ran in and out of the water, barking for her to throw it stones.

Boyd and I both stopped involuntarily on the bank and stared at her. But then the dog saw us and ran barking at the bank. She looked up and saw us—and the spell was gone.

I dropped down to the bed of the stream. She smoothed

out her dress hurriedly and came hesitantly towards us. " Monique Dupont ? " I asked.

She stopped then and frowned in a puzzled way.

I repeated the question. " Are you Monique Dupont ? " I asked.

She opened her mouth as though to speak and then stopped it with her hand. Her eyes widened. She seemed incapable of speech.

I had no doubt in my mind then. And to tide her over the first shock of being enquired for, I told her briefly how her mother had written to me and how I had traced her from Naples to Itri and on to Pericele. I spoke in English. And because her eyes remained wide and wondering, I knew that she understood. " You are Monique Dupont, aren't you ? " I asked again.

She nodded and her lips framed a " Yes." She was standing very rigid, her whole body tensed so that her damp dress clung to her body, making it clear that it was the only clothing she wore. Then suddenly her face crumpled and she began to cry. She sank down on the pebble bed, making no attempt to hide her face, but staring straight at me and crying silently so that the tears streamed down her cheeks without her uttering a sound.

It was horrible.

I had never seen any one cry because a miracle had happened before. She was crying because she was happy. It made me realise, more than words could have done, all that she had suffered.

I went over and sat down beside her on the shingle. She was sitting in a patch of sunlight and the pebbles were hot to the touch. But I didn't notice it. I didn't notice anything but that brown elfin face with the wide full mouth that was quivering now and the grey eyes that no longer looked hurt but were shining through a smother of tears.

I didn't say anything. But at length she broke the silence. " I had almost given up hope of anybody coming. I prayed and prayed. And now you've come and every·

thing is all right. I don't know who you are, but thank you very much for coming." She spoke in English, haltingly, as though it were a forgotten language. "What has happened to Daddy and Pierre?"

I told her and she nodded her head slowly. "But Mamma—she is all right, yes?" I let her know as much as I thought she needed to know. Then she said something which hit me like a jab in the stomach. She said simply, "It will be lovely to see Mamma again, and England and France. I thought nobody would ever come for me—and I prayed each day, many times." She was laughing through her tears.

I did not know what to say. Stuart would be furious. It would complicate everything.

She scooped up a handful of water and washed her face. As she dried her face on the hem of her dress, she was looking at me shyly, her grey eyes big and very bright. I just could not leave her here.

"I was told you were naturalised," I said. "Is that correct?"

She nodded. "It doesn't mean anything though. He made me sign. He said I could not stay unless I became an Italian. I did not see how signing a piece of paper made me an Italian. I am not like an Italian at all." She stared at me and I was silent. Her eyes gradually lost their brightness. "Does that make it difficult?" she asked. "Can't an Italian leave Italy?"

"Look, Monique," I said. "I didn't come to take you back to England. I came just to find out for your mother whether you were still alive and if you were all right."

Her eyes dropped then, the long lids closing over them so that her face was a mask. She did not say anything for a moment and I knew that it was because she could not trust herself to speak. "I am sorry," she said at last. "I was being stupid." She sat for a moment clutching at a handful of pebbles so that the knuckles of her small brown hand, delicate as a pianist's but ingrained with dirt and scarred with work, showed white through the tan. " Is it possible that it be arranged ? " Her voice trembled.

" I'll do what I can," I promised. I dared not commit myself further. I had no idea what the legal difficulties might be. " This man Mancini," I said, thinking of the scene by the ford. " The priest told me he was your guardian ? "

She nodded. " He made Aunt Maria do it. He was determined to have me tied to him legally as well as through need. He said that if she didn't agree, he'd turn me out and I could sell my body for the food I'd need."

" But why did he want you tied to him legally ? " I asked.

She flung back her hair from her eyes with a toss of her head and looked directly at me. " Because he's a beast," she said.

" You mean he beats you ? " I asked.

She laughed at that, and it was not a nice laugh in a young girl. " Yes, because he beats me. But he does not beat me because I have done something stupid or wrong. He beats me because he likes beating me. He wants me. But he won't take me by force. To force me to lie with him would weaken his sense of power. He'll only have me when I crawl to him on my hands and knees and kiss his feet and swear to be his slave, body and soul." The words poured from her, her face white and her voice scarcely above a whisper.

" I have to tell you this," she went on, " so that you can realise how much it means to me to get away from Pericele. He told me this the first time he beat me. He had me wait at table. And as I was serving him—there in front of his wife, he touched me. And when I drew back, he flew into a rage and sent me to my room. Then he came and flung me on the bed and beat me with a bamboo cane. I'm sorry to tell you, but—I've nobody else to tell. His wife—have you seen her ? She hates me, poor thing. He has made life unbearable for her. He has had so many girls in the village. And the priest ignores it because he is very dependent on Mancini for his living."

" Has he beaten you since then ? " I asked.

She nodded. " The least thing will send him into a rage. He hates me because I refuse to do what he wants. The last few times he has hit me standing until I have stripped off my clothes. Sometimes he waits a long time before beating me; just standing and looking at me. But he has never touched me since that first time."

I sat for a moment, completely stunned by what she had told me. The sunlight seemed strangely brittle as a backcloth to the dark thread of her story. It seemed incredible. I was almost prepared to believe that she had made it up in order to persuade me to get her away from Pericele. Then I looked at her face again and saw those grey eyes fixed on me, unhappy because she had told me something that was shameful to her. And I remembered the impression of the primitive that Pericele had made on my mind.

I put my hand over hers to show that I understood. It quivered like the body of an animal that's been trapped. She took her hand away. " I—I don't like to be touched," she said apologetically.

"Why didn't you leave Pericele ? " I asked to hide my embarrassment.

" Where was I to go ? " she asked. " I did run away once. It was after he beat me that first time. That was last winter. It was cold and I had no food. I got as far as Vicovaro. But it snowed that night. And nobody would help me. They thought I was just a dishonest girl who hadn't got a man. It was worse than being at the farm. He came for me next morning and I was glad to go back because I was so cold. I have never tried again. I know what life is like in Napoli. I was afraid Roma would be the same. A city is more lonely than the country. It is more cruel. Here I have friends. They cannot help me, but it is good to have friends. The dogs know me and the children, and there are women like Emma Scafelli here who are kind to me. It helps when you do not belong to nobody."

" You could have married," I suggested.

But she gave a forlorn shake of the head. " There were boys in the village who wanted me. Some would have married me. But it was no good. You do not know what an Italian mountain village is like. People are born and live and die in the village. They are lost if they leave. No man would have dared to marry and stay. Mancini would have ruined him—and his family. It is difficult to make you understand. But a man like Mancini is very powerful in Pericele."

I sifted a handful of pebbles through my fingers. It was strange and quite horrible to hear this kid, who was born in a nice bourgeois environment, talking so matter-of-factly of things with which she should never have come in contact. It was like hearing a little child swearing. And yet despite all her farmyard knowledge of human nature, she preserved an essential air of innocence.

The sound of horses hooves drumming up the dirt bank of the stream made me turn my head. Horse and rider were coming from the direction of Pericele. As they drew near I recognised the thick-set powerful figure of Mancini. The girl had suddenly tensed with a sharp intake of breath.

I got to my feet as the man reined in his small mare on the bank above us. His temper showed in his face as he flung off the horse. He carried a heavy bullock whip and he looked ugly. Boyd bent down and picked up a stone from the bed of the stream. The old woman stood with her bare feet in the sparkling water and a frightened look on her face.

The whip cracked and cut across Monique's back. " *Via! A casa presto!* " he roared. " And you," he shouted at us, his Italian almost unintelligible in his rage, " get off my land, both of you."

He stood on the bank above us—big and angry, like a bull that has been tormented by darts.

" The girl is French," I said. " I am taking her back to her mother in England."

" The girl stays here," he thundered. " She is Italian and I am her guardian."

Monique turned to me. Her face was resolute, re-signed. " Please go," she said. " I was foolish to think that you could take me away. It was kind of you to come. Tell my mother that I am alive and well. Please say nothing—of this."

She had spoken in English. And because he could not understand it infuriated him. " You little *cretina* ! " he stormed. " Get back to the farm or I'll thrash you so that you never walk again."

" I must go," she said. " See, there are others coming. They have guns . . ."

I looked down the track towards the farm. Two men were running along the bank and the barrels of their shot-guns glittered in the sunlight.

" Good-bye," she said.

Then she climbed the bank and began to walk back along the track towards the farm, a lonely slip of a girl, her bare legs white against the black of her miserable dress.

" Now, get off my land," Mancini ordered.

My mind was made up now. " We'll be at the farm at two in the morning," I called after her in English. " Try and meet us outside. If you can't, show a white hand-kerchief at your window and we'll get you out."

She stopped at that, standing very still. She nodded her head and then turned and walked on along the dusty track.

I climbed up the bank with Boyd behind me. Face to face with Mancini I realised what a colossally powerful animal he was. He stood head and shoulders above me.

" I am going to Rome now," I told him. " In a few days time you will hear from my lawyers. If you so much as touch a hair of that girl's head in the meantime I'll have you arrested by the Carabinieri." I mentioned the name of the *Questore* in Rome and added, " He is an old friend of mine."

I saw that I had impressed him. Friends in Italy mean power and he was not so much of a peasant that he did not understand the danger of running up against the

Questore. But the man's temper was so violent that his only answer was to flourish his whip. The leather thong of it cut across my upflung arm and curled with a sting across my back. " *Via !* " he shouted. " *Via !* " And he swore violently.

" You'll regret that," I said. " And remember—beat that girl again and you'll find yourself in the Regina Ceoli prison." I turned and walked back with Boyd up the path to the farmstead and through the fields to the road and the waiting car.

CHAPTER EIGHT

OFF THE VIA ROMA

WE STAYED the night at Vicovaro, slipping out of the *albergo* at one in the morning. We let the Italian driver sleep on. We wanted no witnesses. The moon was low over the mountain tops as we drove the Lancia towards Pericele.

Looking back on it, I suppose it was a pretty crazy thing to do. Kidnapping girls isn't the healthiest of sports, especially in Italy where the jails have a bad reputation. But I don't see what else we could have done. After what she had told me I could not leave her at the farm. And how else was I to get her away? A legal wrangle would have lasted years.

When I broached the matter to Boyd, he said, " Wot the hell ! We didn't conquer this bleedin' country to have bastards like Mancini chuckin' their weight about and beating up girls who should by rights be in Blighty." And he didn't know the full story of what the girl had been through. " Anyway, it ain't as dangerous as you make out," he added. " If we get the kid out orl right, reckon Mancini won't squawk. And the law ain't orl that hot in this land of treasures. I found that out pretty nippy like when we was running the coastal trade. An' I don't reckon it'll have changed much in a couple of years. The Carabinieri ain't paid enough to make it worf their while ter refuse a bribe like wot a London copper is." And he gave me a sly wink.

There was a lot in what he said. The difficulty was going to be to get her out of the farm. I found myself wishing that Stuart was with us and that we had those arms that Dugan had found. If they were waiting for us with shotguns, it wasn't going to be too healthy.

We reached the spot where we had parked the car the

previous morning. I turned and then switched off.
" You'll find the ignition key under the left-hand seat,"
I told Boyd.

Then we went down through the fields to the stream
and along the bank towards Pericele. It was nearly two
when we reached the Mancini farm, a vague huddle of
buildings in the shadow of the trees. The moon had set
behind the mountains now, but the pale light of it still
lingered in the warm summer sky.

We entered the yard of the farm stealthily and stood
in the shadow of an outhouse that smelt of pigs. The
place was very silent. And yet it did not seem asleep.
It had the watchful stillness of a wild thing. The air was
heavy with the rank odours of the farm. But it was not
the smell of an English farm. It was foreign and made
me feel jumpy.

We didn't speak, but stood quite still until the luminous
dial of my watch showed it to be past two.

There was no sign of the girl.

" You stay here," I said to Boyd. " I'll circle the farm
and see if there's a handkerchief at any of the windows."

He said, " Okay," and I moved off along the wall of
the outhouse. My shoes squelched in a morass of wet
dung. I felt the warm heavy-smelling liquid top the
uppers of my shoes. But I dared not try and avoid it.
There was still enough light for me to be seen if I moved
out of the shadow of the buildings. The end of the outhouse abutted on to the farmhouse itself. On this side
there were two small windows on the upper floor. They
were closed and reflected the pale light of the sky like
blind eyes.

Round at the back it was the same. All five windows
were closed and there was no sign of a handkerchief. I
circled the farm until I was gazing at the front door.
This was open. But all the windows on this side too were
shut. There was no sign of life.

I worked my way back to where I had left Boyd.

He was not there.

I thought perhaps I had made a mistake in the growing

darkness. But a little farther on I found the same morass of liquid dung.

A cock crowed.

I felt the menace of the place all round me. One half of my mind was wondering where the hell Boyd could have got to. The other half was detached and thinking about who built the place and what dark scenes the old grey stones had witnessed.

The silence of the yard was shattered by the crash of an iron bar on stone. It sounded as loud as the gates of Hell being thrown back, and a dog began to bark. A door creaked and Boyd and Monique erupted into the yard from the outhouses on the other side. Some one shouted. And then a man's figure appeared in the front of the house. He had a gun. But he did not fire. "*Aspetti !*" he shouted and began to run towards them.

It was Mancini. Even in that dim uncertain light I could not mistake his thick powerful figure.

"Run for the car," I called out to Boyd.

"Okay," he replied, and he and the girl made for the track along the stream bank.

I crouched, ready to do something that I hadn't done in years. Mancini was running across the yard now. Big though he was he ran well, with long powerful strides. As he reached the middle of the yard, I launched myself from the shadow of the outhouse. I made straight for his legs in a flying tackle and caught him nicely at the knees. I felt the solid bone of his leg against my shoulder and then he hit the stone of the yard with a thud that must have shaken him badly.

I dived for the shotgun which had fallen from his grasp. But his hand reached out and fastened on the collar of my coat. He was winded by his fall. But his hold was firm though I struggled desperately. He was breathing in great gulps of air with a sobbing sound in his throat. A moment and he would be fully recovered. I knew I hadn't a hope against him at close quarters.

I kept free of his other hand which was searching for

a hold and wriggled out of my jacket. A quick twist and
I was free.

I reached the gun a moment before he did and then
ran for the track.

He started to run after me. But he was too shaken.
As I made the bank a confusion of shouts broke out
behind me. He was calling for his horse. I settled down
to run steadily and carefully.

I caught up with Boyd and Monique in the fields below
the main road. " Thank God, you're okay, sir," he
panted. " I was a bit worried. 'E ain't hexactly Tom
Fumb's baby bruvver. Wotjer hit 'im wiv—an atomic
bomb ? "

I told him about the tackle. I knew it would please
him. He was a great boy for Twickenham. " Where did
you find the girl ? " I asked as we clambered into the
car.

" She was locked in one of them outhouses," he replied.
" A filthy stinkin' bloody hole of a Calcutta. There was
a little grating winder in it and she'd tied 'er 'anky to it.
I caught sight of it across the yard just after you'd left
me. The draw-bar on the door was secured by a padlock.
But I managed to pick that. Then o' course I went an'
spoilt it orl by dropping the bleedin' bar. Still, orl's well
wot ends well, as ol' Bill would say." He gave me a
nudge with his elbow and speaking out of the side of his
mouth, said, " Cor, stone the crows ! She don't 'alf smell
a treat though. The floor of the place were just like a
ruddy sewer." His nose wrinkled and he grinned. " Pardon my mentioning it, sir, but you don't smell so 'ot
yourself. I 'eard you walk into the muck as soon as you'd
left me. Thort you was going to give the whole game
away by swearing bloomin' orful like wot yer does on the
bridge when somefink's gawn wrong."

The car did in fact smell like a dung heap. I thought
at first it was my shoes. But now I realised that by far
the strongest smell emanated from the back of the car.

I switched the interior light on and looked round. The
girl was sitting close up in the back seat—a tight little

bundle of filth that smiled at me apologetically, her teeth showing white in a dirty face.

" All right ? " I asked.

She didn't speak. She simply nodded. Her eyes were very wide.

I switched the light off and the swathe of the headlights seemed to leap out into the darkness of the winding mountain road again.

As we swung down the mountain road along the valley side to Vicovaro, I tried to figure out how she must be feeling. So far, I realised, I had only been thinking of myself. I had promised to find the girl, and then when I had discovered the circumstances in which she was living I had to satisfy my conscience and intervene. It had— I realised it now—been a game to me. There'd been a brutal farmer to outwit, a risk to be taken. That was all, as far as I was concerned. And afterwards the trouble of getting her back to England.

I hadn't looked at it from her point of view at all.

Her wide eyes and slightly tremulous smile, and the way she sat tense and small in the corner of the car, were eloquent of her state of mind.

And as we drove down through the dark mountains I think I came near to understanding her mood.

However hateful Mancini had been, the farm was at least a home to her. She knew what it was like to be alone and a refugee. The village had given her friends and a background. And then two strangers had come with word of her mother. And now she was alone with them in a car, her dress all covered in filth where she had been flung on to the floor of a dung-strewn outhouse by the furious Mancini—and she was now realising that she did not know these two strangers, did not know whether they could in fact get her back to England, did not know what was to become of her.

Later the trip might seem an adventure to her, for she was young and youth responds to the unknown. But just at the moment she was uncertain and a little scared. With every kilometre the car made down the valley, she was getting farther and farther from the life she knew and nearer and nearer to the outside world. She was intelligent enough to realise that the past few years had not equipped her to cope with that world. It made her very dependent upon us. And dependence upon people you don't know is not very reassuring, even when you're young and leaving a person you detest.

At Vicovaro we stopped just long enough to pick up the Italian driver.

He was very sleepy and disgruntled at being hauled out of bed at four in the morning. As he climbed into the driving seat and smelt the sickly-sweet farmyard stench of the car, he burst into a stream of furious Italian. He spoke so fast and so volubly that neither Boyd nor I could understand what he was saying. But I got the general idea, and I couldn't really blame the fellow. It was a nice car and it would need a lot of cleaning and disinfectant before it was even fit to be hired by a Neapolitan tart.

" You gonna drive or do we dump you here ? " Boyd asked threateningly in Italian.

The stream of words was suddenly damned. He glanced quickly from one to the other of us. ' I drive," he said, and climbed in behind the steering wheel. But as he let in the clutch he started again. " *La mia macchina*," he cried, " *é rovinata*."

" If you're so worried about the way your car smells, why don't you give up eating garlic ? " Boyd suggested. " Yer bref is so bleedin' orful that it's a wonder ter me you notice a nice clean smell like dung."

And whilst Boyd and the driver embarked in this manner upon an amicable chat in front, I sat with Monique in the back and told her about the ship we had at Naples and how if there was any difficulty with the authorities we'd smuggle her out. I told her about Stuart and how we'd got the L.C.T. off the rocks at Bossiney. By the time we ran into Tivoli familiarity with our background was giving her back some degree of confidence.

D.A.

The first pale light of the early summer dawn was showing behind the jagged peaks of the Abruzzi as we swung south on to a side road that led to Valmontone and Route Six.

The flat plain of Rome stretched ahead in the darkness. But by the time we hit the main Rome-Naples highway, with the city well away to our right, it was light enough to see the outline of the Alban Hills.

The sun rose behind the line of the mountains to the east and the trees began to slant their shadows across the road. In the valley of the Sacco we found a gush of clear water falling from the rocks through which the road was cut. We stopped the car and washed ourselves. The fresh morning sunlight was already making the rock warm to the touch.

Until that moment I hadn't really realised what a disreputable trio we looked. Boyd had only the dirt of the outhouse walls on his blue suit. But I was a wreck, my shirt torn from collar to waist, no jacket and no tie. My trousers were rent at the knee and were caked with filth where I had hit the muck of the farmyard. My shoes were covered with a film of dust that had caked on the liquid dung. Beneath the dust, the muck was still wet.

But the girl was in a worse state than any of us. It was on her face and neck and hair. Her legs were caked with it and her dress was indescribably filthy.

Early though it was, the flies swarmed round us, settling on clothes and skin, filling the air with a low hum and driving us nearly frantic with their persistence. The driver watched us nervously. I think he suspected us of being Sicilian gangsters.

I washed my face and hands, and then I washed my shoes. I could do nothing about my trousers but leave the muck to dry on them. When I had finished, I looked round to find the girl standing disconsolately by the car. The toes of her bare feet were dug into the road edge and she did not look very happy.

I glanced across the road. Bushes grew there in the shade of some low trees. " If you go over there and throw

your clothes out to me, I'll wash them for you," I said.
" They'll dry in a few minutes in the sun."

I sensed her relief at the suggestion, though she looked
as nervous as a young deer. A fractional hesitation, and
then she nodded. Her lips started to frame the Italian
" Grazie," but what she said was, " Thank you."

I understood her momentary hesitation when I had
her clothes in my hands. There was only the roughly
patched black dress.

When I had washed it for her, she didn't wait for it to
dry, but put it on damp and came out into the road
again and washed herself, while Boyd and I and the
Italian driver smoked a cigarette and tried to fend off
the flies. I glanced at her once. She was washing her
hair. She noticed me looking at her, shook the hair out
of her eyes, wrinkled her nose and began to laugh.

But I didn't feel like responding. I had just tried to
produce my cigarettes and had suddenly realised that
with the loss of my jacket I had also lost not only my
cigarette case, but my wallet, my cheque book and my
passport.

The cigarette case was a silver one given me by my
mother on my twenty-first birthday. It had been all
through the war with me. The wallet and the cheque
book I didn't really mind about, except of course that
they handed Mancini complete evidence of my identity if
he wished to make trouble. But it was the loss of the
passport that was really annoying. It meant hanging
around at the British Consul's office in Naples in order
to get it renewed.

I felt angry and dispirited. Things seemed to be going
wrong. And my mood was not improved when we eventually climbed back into the car to find it seething with a
million flies and the smell of dung increasingly unpleasant
after the cool dampness of the air in the valley.

Fortunately Boyd had a little money on him and we
were able to buy some food in Frosinone and a pair of
straw sandals and a cheap cotton dress and underwear
for the girl.

She changed into the new clothes behind a stone wall just outside the town. It was staggering the difference they made. The sandals, which were heeled, made her taller and accentuated her long limbs. The bright colours of the cotton print brought out the golden brown of her arms and face, and her small firm breasts, lifted and pointed by a brassiere, thrust impatiently at the cotton of her frock. She had borrowed a comb from Boyd, and her fair hair, combed back from her head, gave her a boyish look.

It was then that I first realised that she was an extremely attractive girl.

She had the black dress in her hand as she came out from behind the wall. She started down the road towards us. But after a few paces she stopped. She looked down for a second at the dress. Then, with a gesture almost of abandonment, she flung it over the wall.

She came towards us then with long, swinging strides. She looked like a Scots girl—very free and easy in her movements. She was smiling as she came up to us as though she had dropped her past over the wall with the black dress.

It was getting hot and the glare of the sunlight as we drove on and lack of sleep made me drowsy. I woke to find Boyd shaking me. "We're just coming to Cassino," he said.

High on our left the battered fragments of the monastery stood white and dusty against the blue bowl of the sky like jagged remnants of a gargantuan tooth. We skirted Monastery Hill through neat little rows of jerry-built Government houses. Down the hill into Cassino proper, we found that nature had moved in on the ruins. The place was covered in dusty greenery. It was no longer impressive.

Somehow I felt deeply disappointed. It should have been preserved as a monument to the folly of man. Once the scarred and battered hillside had been terrifying. Now it was just an untidy jumble of weeds. The same thing had happened in France after the previous war.

I don't know why I hadn't expected it here. Perhaps because there had been so much talk at the time of preserving the ruins as a warning to future generations. But then of course there had been so many other ruins after Cassino—bigger and better ruins. I had only seen Cassino once before—but it had impressed me the same way that the lava of Vesuvius covering Massa di Somma had impressed me. The sun had been setting and I had been in a jeep travelling from Naples to Rome just after the capital had fallen. There had been no living thing in the whole of Cassino then. The crumbled masonry and gaunt fragments of the battered town had stood solitary and lifeless, the stone a warm dull red in the evening light.

As we slid away from it along the dead straight road of the plain below—the same road that had once been the most heavily shelled stretch in the world and had rightly been called the Mad Mile—the weeds in Cassino seemed fair comment in a world that forgets so quickly the death of its sons.

We had a snack at Capua and got into Naples shortly after three in the afternoon. I told the driver to go straight to the docks. I wanted to find out whether Stuart had fixed up a cargo and if so when we were sailing. There was Monique to accommodate and I needed some money to pay for the hire of the car.

But down on the mole I could see no sign of the *Trevedra*. " Shifted 'er berth, I expect," said Boyd. And I must say I wasn't worried. You're always liable to shift your berth in a big port. He might have had to move to take on his cargo.

I went to the Port Authorities office and enquired for the present berth of the *Trevedra*. The clerk glanced at his chart of shipping. " Not there," he said. " Perhaps it's sailed."

" It couldn't have done," I told him.

He glanced down the list of names in his book of sailings. " Here you are," he said. " Sailed 03.30 last night. Destination—London."

A sudden hollow feeling hit me in the stomach. " But that's impossible," I said. " My name is Cunningham. I'm part owner. She can't have sailed. She must be standing off in the Bay."

The clerk wiped a globule of sweat off the end of what would once have been described as a Patrician nose, and looked up at his wall chart again. " No," he said, " it's not standing off. You can see for yourself. There are the names of all the ships that are standing off to-night."

" Probably Mr. McCrae left a note for me then," I suggested.

He looked round at his message rack. The pigeon-hole under C was empty. To his annoyance I had him look at the address of every envelope in the whole rack. But not one was addressed to me.

There was nothing for it then but to go back to the mole and see if any of the stevedores or the crews of other ships moored alongside could tell us anything.

But somehow I knew it was useless. When I told Boyd, he shook his head and said, " It ain't like Mr. McCrae. He's been too long a soldier to leave an RV without notifying the rest where the stragglers' post is going to be."

All we could find out from men working on the mole and from neighbouring ships was that the *Trevedra* had pulled out in the early hours of the morning. I actually interviewed a man who had been on watch on the ship that had pulled in to the vacant berth and his timing of the *Trevedra's* departure confirmed that given me by the clerk at the Port Authorities office.

I tried to ignore the feeling of suspicion that crept into my mind. I couldn't believe that Stuart was crooked. If he had really sailed for England he must have had good reason. But if he had, he was sure to have left a message for me somewhere—at the bank, for instance.

Having reached that conclusion I felt a sense of relief. " How much money have you got ? " I asked Boyd.

" Just over two thousand lire," he said.

And I had a gold wrist-watch. The bank would be

closed now, but I could pop the watch and that would pay the driver. I paid him the full amount I got for the watch. It was safer to overpay him. Then we went to a quiet tenement hotel behind the waterfront where they didn't worry about the fact that we had no baggage.

We fed that night at a little *trattoria* full of tobacco smoke and the sour smell of stale vino. Over the meal I told Monique what I knew of her mother. She listened in silence, her big grey eyes fixed on me. When I had finished, she said, " I shall have to work. Will they take me on a farm ? I am good with animals. They like me."

" Farmin' ain't the sort o' work for the likes of you," Boyd cut in.

She laughed. It was a pleasant musical laugh and it made me feel strangely happy, for it was so light-hearted and gay. " Why not ? " she asked. " I've been a farm girl for over two years now. What other work is it that I can do ? "

What she said was true. There was nothing else she could do. And it was my responsibility that she was leaving the world she knew and going to a strange country that she had only visited twice on holidays. My acceptance of that responsibility produced in me a feeling of tenderness for her—that and the strong wine we were drinking which was *Lacrimo Cristi* from the slopes of Vesuvius. " There's no need to worry," I said. " For instance, you might get a job as interpreter. The French tourist traffic is increasing. Every one in Europe wants to come to England to see the ruins of London. Promise me you won't worry about a job. We'll see you through."

She smiled. I think she knew I was getting a little drunk. " I promise," she said. " And thank you."

I must have been feeling very tired for my mood changed suddenly to one of despondency. " Anyway, before we worry about getting you a job, we've got to get to England," I said. And then I explained to her about the *Trevedra* and how we didn't know what had happened.

" What puzzles me," I continued, turning to Boyd,

" is how he got a crew together in such a short time. He couldn't have sailed her himself. He would have had to sign on a skipper."

Boyd shrugged his shoulders. " It ain't difficult in a big port like this. Though why 'e didn't wait fer us I can't think."

" I should have wired him from Rome," I said. " But he didn't suggest there was any urgency." We had finished our meal now and as Boyd paid the bill, I said, " Anyway, don't let's worry about it. I'll get some money from the bank in the morning and there'll be a letter from him explaining everything. Then we either follow on the next boat or have a pleasant holiday on Capri waiting for the *Trevedra* to come out again."

" What about Miss Monique's papers ? " Boyd asked as we went to the door.

" I'll fix that with the British Consul when I see him in the morning about a new passport," I told him. " It shouldn't be all that difficult."

Outside it was very dark and the streets showed wet in flashes of forked lightning that periodically split the clouds, outlining the mass of the Castello San Elmo towering high above the city. What I had taken to be the sound of traffic, blurred against the hum of conversation in the *trattoria*, had been the distant roll of thunder. The streets were empty. But it was not raining.

I took the girl's arm as we turned down the street towards our dingy hotel. She started at my touch and stopped, her arm withdrawn from mine as though I had hurt her. The lightning forked and I saw her in its photographic flash rigid against the stone of the houses that flanked the street, her eyes wide and startled. Then it was black again and I heard her voice close to me saying, " Please—it is very foolish of me. I am sorry." And I remembered all that she had been through and how she had taken her hand from mine as we sat on the pebble-strewn bottom of the stream.

But instead of showing her that I understood, I said, " You're a strange girl, Monique."

Then it began to rain big summer drops from the heavy sky and we ran for it through the dark streets to the hotel.

Next morning, the rent in my trousers mended and wearing Boyd's jacket which fitted me a little tightly, I presented myself at the Banco di Napoli. I explained that my cheque book had been stolen. The cashier gave me an old-fashioned look and asked me for a specimen signature with a sly grin that was a bit wide of the mark in the circumstances. I also asked him for a letter that I was sure my partner had left for me.

In a few minutes he returned with a new book. " I am afraid there is no letter for you from Signor McCrae," he said. " Here is your new cheque book. I have arranged for no cheques on the old book to be cashed." Gold teeth flashed in his sallow face and the lenses of thick-rimmed spectacles were blind circles of white as they caught the light from the glass roof. " Our clients often lose their books in Napoli. It is a bad city. Often the girls are working for a forger. It is necessary for us to be very careful. Were you thinking of drawing at all, Signor Cunningham ? " I had opened the new book and was on the point of writing out a cheque for twenty thousand.

He had to repeat the question for my mind was struggling to grasp the fact that Stuart had left me no message. " Are you sure my partner did not leave a note for me ? " I asked.

" Quite sure," he said. " They are always left with Signor Borgioli, one of our assistant managers. If you like I will ask the cashiers ? "

I nodded and he went along the counter. I watched him as he spoke to each of the cashiers in turn. One by one they glanced curiously at me and shook their heads.

Then suddenly he was back again with a little man who had false teeth that did not fit and a little pointed beard. " This is Signor Mercedes. He saw Signor McCrae the day before yesterday."

The little man nodded vigorously. " *Si, si*—he was a
tall man with a beard, yes ? He came in the morning
and drew out all the cash in your account except for a
nominal thousand lire."

" He drew out all the cash in our account ? " I repeated.
I couldn't believe it.

" Except for the nominal thousand. He said he had
to pay for a cargo, but would be banking with us again
on the return trip."

" That was why I was asking whether you wished to
draw, signore," put in the first cashier. " It would be
very difficult—impossible. The manager would not
agree—that is except for the thousand lire. You have
only had an account with us for a few days."

" And he left no note—no message ? " I asked again.

They both shook their heads.

There was nothing I could do. I thanked them and
went out into the sunlit roar of the Via Roma.

It was hot and that horrible doubt of Stuart was back
in my mind. There was only one other place in Naples
he could have left a message for me. Guidici's office above
the Galleria Umberto.

I turned left down the Via Roma. It was in the
Galleria that I first realised how desperate our position
was. The sun streamed through the glassless roof and the
heat of it struck up from the tiled paving. But it looked
cool under the gaudy umbrellas of the pavement cafés
where the usual prostitutes sat sipping iced drinks,
waiting to pick up a man or for their pimps to bring a
client to them. I felt the need of a drink badly.

It was then that I realised that I hadn't any money.
I couldn't have a drink. I couldn't even eat. All we had
in the world was the remains of Boyd's two thousand.

I went up the dark stairs to Guidici's office with a foreboding that there would be no message for me. And I was
right.

The secretary shook her dark mop of hair at me
and her eyes fastened like black buttons on the roughly
patched rent in my trousers. I insisted upon seeing

Guidici himself. But there was no message. "Signor McCrae has not been here at all since he came with you about the cargo," he said.

There was nowhere else I could go.

I went back to the hotel and explained the situation to Boyd and Monique. We sat in committee in my room. We called for our bill and found that it left us with just four hundred and twenty-six lire. And Boyd had a cheap wrist-watch. That was all we had between ourselves and starvation.

The prospect was not good.

"I just don't believe a bloke like McCrae would walk out on 'is pals," said Boyd. "Hit ain't in the nature of the man. Stands ter reason like that if a bloke's bin an orficer in the Army as long as 'e was, 'e don't walk out on 'is pals. Dugan wouldn't neither. Jack's as straight as they come."

That's what I thought. But the fact remained that two days ago, whilst we were at Pericele, Stuart had drawn out all our capital and sailed with the *Trevedra*, leaving no message. "Clearly," I said, "since we've no choice, we must work on the assumption that he's left us flat. We need money. And we want to get back to England."

"Reckon it won't be difficult for us to work our passage back," Boyd said.

I glanced quickly at the girl. Her grey eyes met mine and I knew that she had understood. Also I knew that she wasn't afraid. I suppose she was now accustomed to expecting the worst—poverty and uncertainty had been her life for so long.

I said, "There's nothing to stop you working your passage back, Boyd. But I'm not moving from Naples unless I can take Monique back with me."

"Strewf, guvner, you don't think I was suggesting going without her, do you? But I reckoned wiv her knowledge of lingos she might get a job as a stewardess."

We must have talked it over for nearly an hour. "The upshot of the whole thing is," I said finally, "that we must find a cheap place to live and some means of getting hold of some money. Clearly the three of us can't go down to the docks this afternoon and expect to be offered jobs at once in a ship sailing to England."

And this was where Monique suddenly spoke for the first time.

" There is a little place at the top of a house in the Vico Tiratoio where I lived for a time with my aunt. It's not a very nice place. It's a—sort of *pensione*. But the Signora was kind to me and I am sure she would let us have rooms for a time without wanting immediate payment. She often helps people. Sometimes they repay her. Many strange people come there. And there is a Scotch man in the next house—perhaps he is still there. He would help. He is an artist, but not very good. He makes papers for people. And he knows *le monde des apaches*. Many people come to see him for his papers."

We both stared at her in astonishment.

It was difficult to remember that this kid from a mountain farm had lived for three months in one of the worst quarters of the city.

There was nothing else to be done. We paid our bill and followed Monique. After a quarter of an hour's walking I found myself standing outside the *trattoria* in the narrow street above the Via Roma where I had stood only a few days ago, wondering about Monique and the strange life she must have led there.

We climbed the dark narrow stairway which the drunk had climbed, our footsteps sounding loud on the hollow wooden stairs.

And so we found rooms—little cubicle affairs, flimsily partitioned with stained matchboarding and clearly designed for one purpose only. The Signora, a big raddled motherly Neapolitan, welcomed Monique like a long lost child and seemed surprised when we insisted on a separate room for her. I did not like the idea of living in such a place. But we were little better than beggars and could hardly assume the right to be choosers. The Signora did not look impressed at our promises of ultimate payment

—she smiled indulgently, her eyes on Monique with what I thought to be a covetous gleam.

Boyd and I shared a double bed in one cubicle and Monique had the next cubicle to herself. I understood now why she had never even considered trying to get to Naples. If she had come to this house, the Signora would have looked after her for a time. But kindly disposed though she might be to the strange cases that found their way to the top of those wooden stairs, sooner or later she would have insisted on her working for a living. And I could well imagine what hell that would have been to a fastidious girl who did not like being touched.

The *trattoria* down below had an upstairs room for regular clients that was reached by a door at the top of the first flight of stairs. Here you could get food as cheap as anywhere in Naples. The three of us lunched there in the stuffy fly-ridden half-light provided by a grimy window. We lunched well off *pasta asciutta* and red wine for the price of a few lire each.

After lunch I left Monique in Boyd's care and went to the office of the British Consul. With some difficulty I obtained admission to the Consul himself. He eyed me without enthusiasm and did not offer me a seat. If you want a sympathetic Consul, avoid big ports. He listened to my story attentively, but without surprise. When I had finished, he said, "There'll be a little delay, but I can fix you up with a temporary passport. The girl is going to be more difficult. I can get her an Italian passport, but if her guardian notifies the police there may be trouble. Anyway, how do you propose to get her to England if you have no money ? "

He was very off-hand about the whole thing. I could see that he did not believe my story in full. He thought I was entangled with the girl. He was willing to get me a passport, but not anxious to have anything to do with her.

It was useless to protest. I told him not to worry about the girl, but to go ahead with obtaining a temporary passport for myself. I asked him whether there was any

British organisation in Naples through which I could
obtain a loan. His reply was, " I am afraid not. But you
can work your passage back. I'll give you a note to one
of the shipping lines." And he scribbled a line or two on
a sheet of paper, slipped it into an envelope and handed
it to me.

From the Consul's office I went to see the Naval
Liaison Officer. I told him the story and his reaction was
the same as the Consul's. " I can probably arrange for
you both to work your passage home. But to do anything
for the girl is quite out of the question." There were
several other naval officers there, but none that I knew.
I was too embarrassed even to raise the question of a
loan.

Though the sun was now dipping behind the heights
of the Vomero, the streets were still stiflingly hot as I
made my way up into the city. I felt dispirited and
exhausted by the time I reached the Vico Tiratoio. We
were in a bad fix and I didn't see how the devil I was going
to get the girl back to England. And I was definitely not
going to leave her alone here in Naples.

The sweat rolled off me as I climbed the dark stairs,
and I began to swear obscenely and childishly at Stuart.

Boyd and Monique were not in the *pensione*. I went
down to the *trattoria*, thinking they might have decided
to eat. But they were not there either.

I began to walk through the deepening shadows of the
narrow streets. I had a sense of frustration. I was nearly
thirty. And it irked me that at that age I could be
stranded in a foreign city with literally no one to turn to.
It made me realise what a hell of a gap the war had torn
in our lives.

My sense of loneliness made the throng of life in the
drab back-streets more vivid. The film of dirt on the
hairy legs of the girl who shuffled ahead of me in wooden-
soled sandals, the urgent shrill cries of the ageless women
behind the street stands, the beggars, the boys who
wandered barefooted through the streets pimping for
their sisters who were still in their teens, the tawdry

make-up of a woman standing hopefully beneath the
tinsel-decorated lamp-lit shrine of the Madonna at the
street corner, the poverty and the dirt, and the sour
smell of streets that had no proper sanitation—it was all
imprinted on my mind as the background to which I was
doomed until I could fix a passage for the three of us.

And when we reached England, the prospect would
not be very much brighter unless we could get hold of
Stuart. Neither Boyd nor I had a job. I had no money—
no one to whom I could turn for money. And Monique's
mother could hardly support herself, let alone her
daughter.

I felt as depressed as I have ever felt.

The shadows deepened and lights appeared in the
street-level hovels where people not only worked, but
lived. It was the end of the day when the poor of Italy
come out of their shops and their stuffy rooms to sit on
chairs in the street, smoke their last cigarette and gossip.

I walked through street after street where the doors of
the ground-level rooms were open to show the sordid
intimacy of a one-room home with its iron bed and dirty
sheets, a torn stained table-cloth laid with a frugal meal
of *pasta* or *noci* or just *pane*, with the inevitable carafe
of *vino*. And the strange thing was that anybody might
be born to this life. It was just the luck of the draw.
Only a man of character could rise out of this cesspool
of filth if he were born to it—and then he would have to
be either a crook or very lucky.

Without thinking about it I eventually arrived back
in the Vico Tiratoio. I went up to the *trattoria* and found
Boyd and Monique already settled down to plates heaped
with steaming tomato-flavoured *pasta*.

"Strewf! I thort you was lost," Boyd said as he
pulled a chair up for me and shouted for another plate of
pasta.

"You weren't in when I got back so I went for a walk,"
I told him. "Where have you two been—sight-seeing?"

Boyd grinned and glanced across at the girl. "Show
him," he said.

She slipped her hand inside her dress and brought out a bulky envelope. She handed it to me almost shyly like a child that has done something that it fears is wrong but hopes will be approved.

Inside were some papers and a slim book. The papers were civilian identity documents. The book was a passport visa'd for England.

" How the hell did you get this ? " I asked. I spoke sharply. I was excited and at the same time angry. The passport photograph had been taken that afternoon, for it showed her in the print dress we had bought her in Frosinone.

Boyd answered for her. " They're forged," he said. " But they'll do in an emergency. The way I look at it is this. The bloke offered ter do it. Why should we refuse ? If we did get her a berf as a stewardess we'd be pretty mad if it fell through because she 'adn't got the necessary papers."

" Who was this forger ? " I asked.

Boyd was about to reply when Monique said, " Please. You remember I told you I knew a Scotch man who——"

" Scotsman," I corrected her automatically.

" Yes—a Scotsman who was kind to me when I was here before ? We went to him this afternoon. He is now very ill—his legs will not walk . . ."

" He's paralysed," Boyd interrupted. " Got a packet in Naples after he deserted. This Goddammed city's full of disease."

" He's a deserter and he forges passports and papers for all the crooks in Naples—is that it ? " I asked.

" He is an artist," Monique said. " I don't know what is a deserter. He does work for many bad people. He is not a good man. But he has been a friend to me. And when I told him that we had no money and wanted to get to England and that I had no papers or passport, he made them. He is very ill," she added as though that explained everything.

" We're going to his studio to-night for a drink," Boyd said. " He says he thinks he can help us."

"Well, I'm not," I said. I felt angry—humiliated. "You say the man is a deserter, a forger, and diseased. Even Monique says he is not a good man. Why did you take her there?"

Boyd looked aggrieved and shrugged his shoulders. "I weren't in no position to stop 'er. The young lady's got a mind of 'er own. Anyway, it won't do no 'arm to look in. He's friendly—and we ain't hexactly overburdened wiv friends at the moment. Besides, he said he'd give us some Scotch, an' speaking for meself I could do wiv a nice drop of Scotch."

I shrugged my shoulders. I was too depressed to argue. And what Boyd said was true. Any straw was worth clutching at.

CHAPTER NINE

THE MAN WHO WAS PARALYSED

THE SO-CALLED artist's studio was on the top floor of the next house. The door at the head of the dark wooden staircase was opened to our knock by a skinny little urchin of about twelve. As soon as we entered the apartment, it was obvious that, though he lived in a slum, he was not short of money. We were shown into a big room with french windows open on to a terrace where evergreens stood in pots half screening a view that ranged across the moonlit rooftops of Naples to the sugar-loaf bulk of Vesuvius.

The shadows were deep in the room. The cold half-light of the moon filtered in to show it expensively furnished in appalling taste.

" *Alfredo! Accendi la luce per favore.*" The voice was soft and slurred.

The urchin went back to the door and the light switch clicked, flooding the room with a golden glow from a big standard lamp in the far corner.

It showed a room furnished partly in the ornate gilt so beloved by the Neapolitan and partly as an artist's studio. There was a low easel near the window, a litter of paints and brushes and palettes on a table, and a desk with a glass top and a base of chromium.

The man we had come to see was seated in a rubber-tyred wheel-chair at the far end of the room. He had a gaudy coloured rug wrapped round his legs and his hands plucked nervously at the covering with long white fingers, the nails of which were grimed and stained with acids. His head was small and nearly bald and his features emaciated. The birdlike impression he gave was accentuated by the quick thrust forward of his head as he said,

" Good-evening. I am glad you have come. I do not often get visits from my own countrymen."

He thrust his wheel-chair towards us with deft movements of his strong hands. A jerk of his head I took to indicate that we should seat ourselves on the uncomfortable gilt chairs. Beads of sweat glistened on his lined forehead. Sharp pale eyes beneath sandy eyebrows suggested that he was no fool and I found difficulty in suppressing a feeling of suspicion.

As though in answer to an unspoken query of mine, he said, " I suppose you are wondering why I have asked you here to-night ? " He pushed a box of cigarettes across to us. It was a wooden box, the top inlaid with a picture of Vesuvius. " Help yourselves," he said, and then called, " Anna ! "

The woman who answered his call was as typically Neapolitan as the furniture. She had probably been beautiful only a few years ago. Neapolitan girls are at their best between the ages of sixteen and twenty. She was about twenty-five now—heavy, raddled and slatternly. Only the eyes were still beautiful. They were big and dark, and they watched him like a bitch watching its master. Her legs, though sheathed in silk, were too fat in the calf and she stood with them slightly apart. Her hips were wide and her body heavy. Her breasts, which no doubt had once been firm, were like two great sacks that not even an Italian brassière could support in decency below the low-cut satin dress. Her fleshy features were framed in an untidy mop of jet black hair.

" Bring some drink in," our host ordered. He was massaging the grime from his neck with the tips of his fingers abstractedly, as though considering the line he was going to take with us.

When the woman had brought glasses and a bottle of whisky and he had poured all of us, including Monique, a nearly neat drink, he said, " Yes, I think you must be wondering why I asked you to come. You, Cunningham, are also probably wondering why I gave Monique the papers and passport she needed and which you could not get for her."

I did not say anything, but waited for him to go on. The liquor, which was real Scotch, was fiery in the heat of the room.

"It's not out of friendship," he snarled, suddenly darting his slight body forward at me and gripping the wheels of his chair so hard that the backs of his brown hands were almost white. "Nor is it out of sympathy for the jam you're in. You're an officer—or you were. You represent everything I hate about Britain. Do you think I've enjoyed living in exile all these years? I was born at Ballachulish in the Western Highlands. I've forgotten my native dialect. I've almost forgotten how to speak ordinary English. You and your type put me where I am." He leaned back, suddenly relaxed. The sweat was streaming down the sides of his face. He mopped it off with a dirty hankerchief.

"I didn't even ask you here to gloat," he added, softly. "I asked you here because I need your help."

He leaned forward and poured Boyd and myself another stiff tot. "There's a lot wrong with your type of world, Cunningham. But I'll give 'em this—they'll drive men to death in their capitalist wars or in the sweat shops from which they get their money, but they'll always see that they're buried decently. And that's what I want you to do for me." He snickered. It was a sound that might have appeared foolish if it had not been so full of bitterness.

"I don't quite follow you," I said.

His lips twisted back from brown rotting teeth. "I'm not asking favours, Cunningham," he said. "You and your kind won't get that final satisfaction." He leaned quickly forward again. "I'm not wanting your charity. I've been in Wales. I've worked in the anthracite pits, where men die of silicosis because the owners won't take steps to instal modern machinery to keep the dust down. I've seen how charity works. I became a communist then. Now I'm a realist. But I still remember. And if you've got a conscience, I'm not going to help you salve it. Mine is a straight business deal. You help me and I'll help you. Boyd here told me how you were fixed this afternoon. I know something that you don't know. And in exchange for that information you're going to swear to do something for me."

He began to cough then, quietly and chokingly till his whole frame was aflame and the veins on his forehead stood out in ridges.

At length the spasm passed and he sat back weakly. He reached for his glass, drained the neat whisky at a gulp and poured himself another. " I guess it shakes your sense of decency that a nice girl like Monique knows any one like me." He laughed quietly to himself. " Perhaps you're right. Perhaps she shouldn't have known me. She used to come and sit here for hours watching me paint when she lived next door with the Gallianis. I wasn't in this bloody chair then. I don't know why she came. Probably because she was lost and lonely and a stray. If there had been no war and she had lived with her revoltingly bourgeois family, she would never have come anywhere near me. As it was we were both strays, and I suppose that is what we had in common."

He propelled his chair over to the far corner of the room and returned with a medium-sized canvas. It was a portrait of Monique—very sweet and placid and at ease. " That's the best portrait I ever did. I'm not a very good artist. My notes are all right, but my pictures are not good. Except this one—it's got all the longing for my youth and the innocence of first love and the nice clean straight things of life. At least that's what I think. Anyway, that's why I liked having her around. One remembers sometimes. And the last four years are not good company in one's thoughts."

He poured out more Scotch, filling his own glass almost to the brim with neat whisky. " Mostly I try to forget," he went on, raising his glass with a sardonic smile. " But Monique was like a breath of fresh air in a stale room. When she was here I felt young again, forgot

that I was a rotting outcast and remembered my youth
and what I might in different circumstances have made
of my life."

"What do you want me to do?" I asked. "And what
is the information you're willing to trade?"

"Not so fast," he said. The liquor was making his
speech very difficult to follow. "You're one of the so-
called officer class. You're down and out. And I'm the
only person who can help you. That's never happened to
me before. You can sit there with a sneer on your face
drinking my whisky—all right, I am gloating. But
you're going to stay sitting there whilst I tell you just
what you and your sort have done for me. I'm going to
tell you the sort of dirty bastard you've made me." He
laughed. "I've never told a soul. Nobody knows who I
am. Here they all think I'm a Swiss from one of the
French cantons. I'm Signor Buisson." He looked across
at Monique and the bitterness of his face softened
momentarily. "I've told her more about myself than
I've told any other living soul," he said.

He leaned forward to pour out more liquor. Both
Boyd and I refused. We hadn't finished our last glass.
"So I'm not good enough to drink with, eh?" He filled
our glasses to the brim. "Well, you're bloody going to
drink with me. And you're going to listen." His voice
dropped as suddenly as it had been raised.

"My mother still lives in Ballachulish. She'd be about
seventy now. I write to her regularly. She thinks I have
a flourishing little business here in Naples and that I'm
married to an Italian girl and have a kid. Well, it's all
got a basis of truth. This business flourishes all right.
And I've got this woman and the kid, who is a bastard
of hers and nothing to do with me. Whatever else I'd
do, I'd never give even a slut like that——" and he
nodded in the direction of the door through which the
woman had appeared—"a child, the way I am. I'm
going to stop writing to my mother now. I'll be dead
soon anyway. My mother is about the only happy
memory I have left and I don't want her ever to know

what her son was really like—what he did and how he lived. It would break her heart, for my father is dead and I was her only child. That's what I want you to do for me. She's always asking me in her letters when I am coming home to see her. I shall never go, of course."

He sat back and gazed out of the windows. He didn't expect any comment and I said nothing. Words were tumbling into the man's mouth from the depths of his being. I didn't like him. But I felt sorry for him.

"I last saw her when I was twenty-four," he said softly. "That was nearly eight years ago. When I was sixteen my father, who kept a little store in the town, sent me to work with the British Aluminium people. But I wanted to be an artist. I spent all my spare time drawing and painting. I saved some money and got myself to Paris, where I learned little about painting and a lot about how to exist on next to nothing. Eventually I got desperate. I am not a very good artist. I know that now. I went back to England and was in and out of labour exchanges until I joined the Army."

His voice drifted on, a dull monotone in the heat of the room.

It wasn't a new story to me. A lot of men had gone the same way in the moral collapse of a world in chaos.

Frustrated, and suffering from an inferiority complex because he had the sense to know his limitations in the only thing he wanted to do, he found himself posted to Ordnance Survey as a draughtsman. This carried him through the first two years of the war. Then he had been fool enough to seduce his officer's girl friend. Justified or not, he had then developed persecution mania. To get out of the unit he had applied for a commission. After three months at an O.C.T.U. he had been returned to unit. He explained that by saying, "Not the right schools, old man." But then added, "Anyway, gunnery wasn't my line of country at all." Soon after returning to his unit, his officer had had him posted. And to justify the posting he had been given an adverse report.

Within two months he had found himself in an infantry

replacement draft bound for Egypt via the Cape. Too late for Alamein, he had gone into Sicily with Montgomery's Eighth Army.

But though he was realistic enough about his artistic abilities, he had by then developed the artistic temperament to the nth degree. He revolted against the whole life of the infantryman. " It wasn't my sort of job," he said. " Why, because they wouldn't give me a commission, should they shove me in the infantry ? I just wasn't cut for out it. The end came at Cassino. Have you ever been scared—so scared that you feel like blowing your brains out rather than face it any longer ? No, I suppose you wouldn't. You went to the right schools and they taught you to be more afraid of being scared than of hell itself.

" Well, I wasn't made that way. I just cracked up like a lot of other lads. It was in the early spring of '44. We were going out on patrol for the third night in succession. We were platoon strength when we went out and half the lads were crying. It's all so vivid even now. The tears were hot in my eyes and cold on the tip of my chin. I was crying like a child. I just couldn't go through with it. We were going up to the Hotel des Roses to try and wipe out a spandau position that had been worrying us and I just lay on the hard rubble of a ruined building and let the tears stream down my face. I couldn't control myself."

He laughed mirthlessly, drained his glass and refilled it.

" The officer came over to me," he continued. " Give him his due, he did his best to get me to go on. And then when he found I wouldn't, he dug his pistol into my ribs. But I was past caring. ' Go on, shoot me, you swine,' I said. But he didn't. He just sent me back and the next day I was up before the C.O.

" I was sent to a field punishment camp. I didn't care after that. I had no pride left. I escaped and made my way to Naples. I had no money, so I joined up with a gang of deserters who were doing all right. We made a living by pinching trucks and running foodstuffs for the

Black Market. But it was dangerous work and I soon discovered that there was a good living to be made as a forger. For the first time in my life I found myself making money as an artist. Remember the forged greenies and blackies that were turned out. I did the original designs for one of the gangs in that racket. And then there were passes, certificates, passports, licences. I've copied practically every Allied and Italian permit. I've built up one of the most prosperous—and incidentally one of the safest—underground jobs in Naples."

He wiped the sweat off his forehead. He had been talking hard and the liquor was making him a bit dazed. " I've made money, had all the women I wanted, enjoyed life—and I've hated myself doing it. I might have snapped out of it if I hadn't got tied up with Anna the first few weeks I was in Naples. You wouldn't think it now but she was a beauty then, luscious like a fully ripe peach. But she was a tart and she had just bought her way out of hospital for fifteen thousand lire. I didn't know that. I guess I was a fool, but there you are. And now when I've got the money I can't go back to Ballachulish. Not because I'm a deserter—a false name and false papers would be easy. But I'd have to tell her the whole story. And a woman's got a right to end her days in a fool's paradise, thinking she's given birth to a child that's made a position for itself in a foreign land—instead of to a monstrosity, twisted mentally and physically."

He laughed loudly and obscenely, and I saw Monique wince. Then he leaned forward and stabbed an uncertain forefinger at me. " That's where you come in," he said. " The old lady's suspicious. She thinks that if I'm doing as well as I say in my letters there ought to be no reason why I shouldn't take a holiday and go and see her. You must go and see her when you get back to England. Tell her you've seen me. Tell her anything you like about me—anything, that is, except the truth. And tell her I'm dead. Tell her I was run over—an accident. Tell her you saw it happen and were with me when I died in hospital. I'll forge all the necessary papers, including a

will, and I'll have a firm of lawyers send her a legacy.
Tell her that I spoke of her with my dying breath and that
you promised to come and see her. You're the officer
type—she'll believe it all coming from a bloke like you.
She won't expect an ex-naval officer to be lying, will she ?
She'll believe you. That way she'll never know the truth.
She'll never know how I'll really die."

" You can't do this," I said. " It's horrible."

He laughed at that. " Horrible ! Who are you to
judge whether it's horrible or not. A mother will forgive
anything, but not her son mucking around with bad
women. You'll be doing a great kindness. And you'll
do it because you're in a fix and you've made yourself
responsible for the girl here."

I said, " I'd do it anyway if I were convinced it were
the right thing to do. I don't need a bribe to do a kindness for some one."

" You don't need a bribe, eh ? " he sneered. " Well,
you're bloody getting one, whether you like it or not.
I wouldn't trust any one to do this for me unless I held
their conscience in fee. You'll do it for me because it is a
bargain between us—not as a damned kindness. Didn't
I tell you I wouldn't take charity. I've fallen low—Goddammed bloody low—but not as low as that."

He propelled his chair forward until his face was so
close to mine that I could smell his liquored breath and
sweaty body. " Would it interest you to know that I
forged papers two days ago for a tank landing craft ? It
is a strange coincidence that they should come to me,
except of course that I've got something of a corner in
this sort of business around these parts. And would it
interest you to know that the original papers were made
out in the name of *Trevedra* ? "

I stared at him in amazement. At first I could not
believe it. But he had nothing to gain by lying. " You
mean you forged papers for my own ship ? "

He nodded, his lips drawn back in a sneering grin.

" Who did you forge them for ? "

" I never divulge the names of my clients. That is a

cardinal rule in this sort of game. She was purchased by
an Italian firm from McCrae for the coastal trade. She
is now known by an Italian name. I know what she is
now called. And, moreover, I know where she is lying
up at this moment."

"It's fantastic !" I said. I was just thinking aloud.

He shrugged his shoulders. "If you live a little
longer in Naples," he said, "you will get used to the
fantastic."

"Tell me one thing," I said, "did they buy her for
running arms ? "

He did not answer my question, but shouted for
Anna again. "Bring my Bible and another bottle,"
he told her. When they arrived he poured us out more
drinks. Then he said, "I'm still Presbyterian enough to
believe that a man who makes an oath with his hand
laid upon the Book will not break faith. Put your hand
on the Book, man, and repeat after me."

I hesitated. But there was no point in refusing. He
would die sooner or later, and it would not be a pleasant
death. Who was I to judge whether his decision was
right or wrong. It would serve no purpose for his mother
to know the truth about his life. And whatever the man
had done—and I had no doubt that he had told us but a
tithe of the rottenness that had been in his life—at least
he had this one spark of decency, that he wished his
mother to die in the belief that her son was the son she
had known eight years ago. It was difficult to refuse to
do what he asked. It would be refusing perhaps the one
decent gesture he had made during the past few years of
his life.

"All right," I said. "But please understand that,
apart from the information you can apparently give me,
I would have done this anyway if you had wished it this
way."

He clicked his tongue. "Never mind about your high
and bloody mighty principles, Cunningham. Just place
your hand on the Book and repeat after me : ' I swear by
Almighty God and all that I hold dear to me, to visit

your mother and tell her of your death and carry to her whatever last messages you direct.' "

I repeated it after him. And when I had finished, he said, " And may the curse of my body rest upon you if you fail to fulfil this charge."

He sat silent for a moment after that. Then at length he said, " And now you'll be wanting to know where your ship is." He spun his chair round and propelled it over to a desk in the far corner of the room. He pulled a sheet of paper from a drawer and for a moment or two the silence of the room was broken only by the scratching of his pen across the surface of the paper.

Then he slid back silently across the room to me and handed me the sheet. " That is my mother's address at Ballachulish and her name. Below it I have put the location of your ship, the name of the man who was behind the outfit that ' acquired ' her and also the name of a *trattoria* and a time. That time is for to-morrow. Go to the *trattoria* and I will have a man meet you there. He is known as *Il Piccolo Polipo*. That means The Little Octopus. He will help you. The people who have acquired the ship want her for running arms. They represent Big Business and neo-Fascism. I am surprised that you did not get on better with them. They would have paid you good money for the ship rather than take the risk of stealing it. The man you will meet at the *trattoria* calls himself a communist. But I think you would find difficulty in understanding his political ideology. He heads a band of men who were once of the *partigiani*. It would not be good for him if neo-Fascism became too powerful in Napoli. He will wish to know where the leader is. Tell him he will be for the next three days at the villa of the banker, Mordini, on Monte Argentario. In return for that information I will see that he helps you to get your ship back. It is in any case to his advantage. If they have that ship for running arms then they will be all-powerful in this area—that is underground. But then the underground is not so far off the surface in this city as it is in most others."

But I was scarcely listening to what he said. I had opened the folded slip of notepaper. In spidery copperplate writing the name Del Ricci caught my eye.

And immediately everything fell into place.

I felt a great relief. It is not nice to be forced to consider a friend no better than a crook.

The location of the *Trevedra* was given as Porto Giglio. " Where is Porto Giglio ? " I asked him.

" It is a port on the island of Giglio about twelve miles off the coast just south of Elba," he said. " *Il Piccolo Polipo* will arrange for a boat and also transport up to Santo Stefano, which will be your port of embarkation." He passed his hand wearily across his brow. " When you see my mother, tell her that it was to-day I died." He looked across at the girl. " Good-bye, Monique," he said. " Pray for me sometimes. And if it's any satisfaction to you, your visits brought light into the darkness of this room. I am glad to have had some part in getting you back to your mother."

She went across to him and took his hand. Then she bent quickly and kissed his forehead.

We left then. And in the moonlit street outside I saw that she was crying. " He was kind," she said, not troubling to hide her tears. " He was kind and he was lonely."

CHAPTER TEN

THE LITTLE OCTOPUS

THE NEXT MORNING at twelve-thirty I went alone to the *trattoria* in the Vicoletto Berio. I sat at an empty table and ordered a glass of *vino*. Shortly afterwards a swarthy man with aquiline features came over from the bar. "*Permesso, Signore,*" he said and sat down opposite me.

He asked me my name. And when I told him and had shown him the piece of paper on which the location of the *Trevedra* had been written the night before, he told me what I had to do. He spoke softly and naturally. " I have been waiting to get this Del Ricci for a long time," he said. " At his villa at Posilipo he has too many of his friends around him. But now he has gone into the country and his friends are not with him. I was told that you would tell me where he was ? "

"He is at the villa of Mordini, the banker," I said. Then, remembering what I had been told the previous night, I added, " The villa is on Monte Argentario."

" Good ! " he said. " That is very good. I know where it is. It is near Santo Stefano and that is where we must embark for the Giglio. We shall leave to-night. How many of you are there ? "

I told him three. " Myself, one of my crew and a girl."

He nodded as though that was what he had expected. " Be outside the Castello Nuovo at midnight where the road comes up from the docks. You cannot mistake it. There is a bridge over the road. A truck will come up from the docks. It will be a five-ton Fiat. I shall be on it. Don't worry if it is a little late. We shall have flour to load. You will know the truck because the driver will switch his headlights on and off three times as he comes up the hill. If all goes well the ship will be yours again the following night. You must be prepared to sail as soon

as she has been liberated." His lips twisted on the word
" liberated " into a sardonic smile. " Is it agreed ? "

When I nodded, he got to his feet. " *Arrivedela,
Signore*."

And that was how it was fixed. I didn't know his
name, what he was or who he was. Just a drink in a café
and everything had been arranged without my lifting a
finger. I was left with a feeling of astonishment. I was
not accustomed to the underground organisation of
foreign ports.

When I told Boyd the plan, his reaction was the same.
" I don't get it," he said. " This bloke Del Ricci pinches
our ship. There's another bloke around the joint who
hates his guts. An' just because we can tell 'im where
this Del Ricci is, he's prepared to act as Santa Claus an'
get the bleedin' ship back for us." His small leathery
face was puckered with bewilderment as he shook his
head and said, " Stands ter reason a bloke'd want payment for a thing like that, especially in this God-forsaken
country. But there ain't no point in our worrying about
it like, is there ? I mean, we ain't got nothink to lose."

He was right there. The only thing I'd got to lose was
my life—or my liberty if we were arrested for attempting
to seize by force something that really belonged to us. I
had no illusions about what was going to happen. The
Little Octopus wasn't taking an interest in us out of
kindness. This was gang warfare and the party wasn't
likely to be a picnic.

We were at the Castello Nuovo shortly before midnight.
It was almost cool with a slight breeze coming in from
the sea. The great square bulk of the castle crouched
black against the moonlit waters of Naples Bay, and
beyond it the dim outline of Vesuvius was raised towards
the sky.

I glanced down at Monique, who was standing beside
me, the sweep of her fair hair stirring gently in the breeze.
I was wondering what she thought about it all. She
sensed my gaze and smiled up at me. There was no fear
in her eyes.

For some reason that annoyed me. "We're going to have trouble on this trip," I told her.

"Do you mean there will be a fight?" She nodded her head seriously. "But you will get your ship back." And she smiled up at me happily again as though life were as simple as all that.

Then the truck came snoring up the road from the docks, its headlights flickering yellow in the white light of the moon.

The Little Octopus leaned out of the driver's cab as it pulled up. "Get in the back," he said, "and make yourselves comfortable. It will be a long drive."

He was quite right about that. The truck was heavily loaded with sacks of flour and made at best not more than twenty miles an hour. There were two Italians in the back. They had settled down to the boredom of being jolted around throughout the night. They nodded as we climbed aboard. But they did not speak. As we topped the hill out of Naples and the sprawling outline of Capri was lost among the trees that lined the road, I adjusted the sacks on which we were resting so that Monique could sleep comfortably. Then I settled myself beside her.

I lay awake for some time watching the trees sweep past and gazing at the tapering vista of the road behind us running like a white sword across the country. Then gradually my senses dulled to the roar of the engine and I dozed off.

It must have been an hour or so later that I woke with a feeling that one of the sacks had fallen across me. I tried sleepily to push it away. My hand touched warm soft-curving flesh and I woke to find it was Monique and not a sack.

She had slipped over on to me with the jolting of the truck. Her shoulder was pressed into my belly and her face, with eyes serenely closed and lashes black against the pale skin, was on my chest. I didn't move my hand from the curve of her breast. I just lay quiet for fear that I should disturb her. If she woke she would be scared at the touch of my hand. And I knew in that moment, with the perception one often has when one has just woken up, that I didn't want her to be scared. I only wanted her to lie there and to feel the warmth of her against my body, to feel the woman of her and pretend that she was lying there because she wanted to.

But some sixth sense must have warned her that I was awake. Suddenly her eyelids flickered open like shutters and her grey eyes, wide and startled, were looking up into mine.

There was no time to take my hand from her breast or to close my eyes and pretend that I was asleep.

She stared up into my face for a moment. Then suddenly she smiled. It was a warm slow luxurious smile—a smile that acknowledged all there has ever been between a man and a woman. She put her hand over mine where it held her breast. Then, still smiling, she closed her eyes and went to sleep again.

I didn't dare move for a long time after that. I just lay there, my whole body conscious of the shape of her, thinking about her and about the future. For she had suddenly become very important to me.

In the end I fell asleep. And when I woke again the sun was up and she was sitting against the tailboard combing the flour out of her hair with a comb she had borrowed from Boyd.

We stopped for a snack at a *trattoria* just outside Rome. And then we drove on as the sun climbed the blue bowl of the sky. It was past midday before we turned off the main road and dipped down through Orbetello, with its shattered seaplane base where Balbo had set off on his record-breaking flight, to the causeway that joins Monte Argentario to the mainland.

The sea on either side of the causeway was white like a mirror. A line of telegraph poles strode across it like men on stilts wading to the shore and bamboo fish pens cut the water into sections as hedges separate fields.

The truck bore right along the northern shore of the peninsula. The road deteriorated into a track bull-dozed

D.A.

two years ago through demolition rubble and the interior of the truck became hazy with flour as the sacks rocked and bounced. Then suddenly it was dark. The temporary road had taken to the railway and we were in a tunnel.

In the sunlight again we climbed a headland and below us lay Porto Santo Stefano, a hillside of brown stone ruins crumbling to the brilliant blue of the sea where the astonished masts of a sunken schooner showed bare and and white.

The little port was smashed to hell and had never been rebuilt. Yet there was a strange beauty in its ruins, for the empty shells of what had once been houses showed the red and blue and green of painted interiors. Here, against the brown of the broken stone, was every colour of the rainbow. The effect was of an artist's palette.

We did not go into the port, but dropped down the shoulder of the hill to a broken concrete jetty where an island schooner was moored stern-on to the hard of what had once been the waterfront. Here the truck stopped and we climbed stiffly out. The two men who had been with us in the back lowered a sack of flour over the tail-board. It hit the concrete with a heavy metallic thud.

The Little Octopus shepherded them aboard across the plank that was roped from the hard to the stern of the schooner, and we followed him. He introduced us to a watery-eyed old ruffian. This was the skipper. His breath smelt of garlic and he spat tobacco juice on to the decks that were high with the smell of fish and *vino* and salt water. Grey hair stood out on the dirt-lined scrawny skin of his neck like stubble and his teeth were black stumps in a framework of cracked lips and brown-stained straggling moustache.

We had a meal in a cabin below decks that was so stiflingly hot that I could feel the sweat trickling down the sides of my body. There were anchovies and olives and tasteless Mediterranean fish with brown bread and a lobster and hard cheese, all washed down with Aleatico from Elba.

When we had finished, the Little Octopus advised us to get some sleep on deck. "You'll be sailing at midnight," he said. "And you'll need to be fresh."

The flour from the lorry was being loaded. The Little Octopus, with his two henchmen, their pockets bulging suspiciously, disappeared with a fishing net in a small boat.

Monique and I stood against the wooden bulwarks of the schooner and watched the boat till the dhow-like sail disappeared beyond the headland.

"Where is he going?" Monique asked.

I shrugged my shoulders. I did not know. But I had an uneasy feeling that necessity was getting us mixed up in something pretty unpleasant. We went for'ard and joined Boyd under the shade of a sail that had been roughly rigged as an awning.

It was a long and boring wait, periodically relieved by the skipper insisting on our taking a glass of wine with him.

But at last the light faded out of the sky and he began to stir his crew to action. The ropes were slipped and the diesel engine throbbed into life. No sails were set. We slipped out round the jetty and made for the headland on our auxiliary engines, though there was a cool breeze whipping at the flat surface of the sea.

We hugged the shore very close in, the cliffs, dark above our bare masts, throwing back at us the monotonous chug of the engine. Beyond the headland was a cove and then another rocky spur with a monstrous villa showing a white sprawl on the edge of its cliffs. The slight swell creamed white against the rocks and as we passed we heard the sound of it breaking. The engines slowed and then suddenly ceased. All was quiet as we slid silently through the water into a little bay.

Gradually the schooner lost way until it was motionless, rocking gently, its up-curved bows facing in towards the dark mass of land that was folded round the bay.

"Wot the heck are we waiting for?" Boyd asked me.

I didn't know for certain. " I think we're waiting for
the Octopus and his mate," I said. An uneasy feeling
crawled through my stomach. I remembered his dark
eyes and thin swarthy face across the table of the *trattoria*
as he said, " I have been waiting to get this Del Ricci
for a long time."

The silence became oppressive. I asked Boyd for the
time and he showed me the luminous dial of his wrist-
watch. It was well past midnight.

The skipper was getting restive. He kept on putting
his hands to his eyes like binoculars and staring towards
the shore where the white of a small building showed
uncertainly at the water's edge.

Suddenly one of the crew caught at his arm and pointed
across our port beam. The dim outline of a boat was
taking shape against the blank darkness of the water.
It came on towards the schooner silently, its oars muffled.
A line snaked through the air as the boat came under our
stern. As soon as it was made fast, the engines were
started again and the schooner swung slowly seaward,
trailing the boat in the froth of its wake.

" Why ain't they comin' aboard ? " Boyd asked me
in a whisper.

I glanced at him. He looked tense and nervous. I
could see that his suspicions were the same as mine. I
moved towards the stern to have a closer look at the
boat. Monique started to come too. But I told her to
wait. I didn't want her involved in it. She was still an
Italian national and the less she knew about it the
better.

Boyd followed me to the stern rail. My eyes were
accustomed to the darkness now and I could see the
interior of the boat quite clearly. The Little Octopus
and his two henchmen were sitting on the thwarts. The
sail was tumbled over the bottom of the boat. It was
humped up as though draped over a sack. But protruding
from one corner of it was the tip of a shoe.

Boyd had seen it too. He whistled softly and muttered,
" Cor ! Ain't there no law in this bleedin' country ? "

We went back to where Monique was standing, her face lifted to the freshening breeze and her hair streaming out behind her. The crew had begun to set the mainsail.

" The less we know about to-night's work, the better," I told Boyd. " We can't do anything about it. This set-up lives outside the law. I suppose it's not unlike Chicago in the twenties. They take that chance. If a man decides to live like a rat there's not much point in being squeamish about his dying like one."

Boyd sniffed. " Makes yer wonder why humans was ever born though, don't it ? " he muttered.

When we were well clear of the land the boat was hauled in alongside and the three men climbed on to the deck of the schooner. I glanced at the boat as it was allowed to drop astern again to the extent of its tow rope. The sail was neatly stowed and it was empty.

We had a beam swell now and the schooner began a dipping corkscrew movement. One of the crew had brought a guitar on deck and the hands gathered round, running through the usual repertoire of Neapolitan songs. Their voices mixed in strange harmony with the slatting of the canvas and the heavy creaming swish of the water thrust aside by the pointed bows.

This did not seem the setting for a murder.

Despite the breeze, the air was warm. Behind us the Apennines were showing a dark ridge in silhouette against the yellow light of a moon that had not yet risen. It was enchanting.

I was thinking how Italy had lost the war. This was the sort of setting that made the Italians an excitable pleasure-seeking race that lived for the moment with no thought for the future, believing in the form of things rather than the substance. As a rather exotic Contessa had remarked to me shortly after the fall of Rome—" We have the Sun and the Moon and Love, what more should we want." The practical demand of the fascists for colonies was out of character.

Monique's voice broke in upon my thoughts. " I can't

believe it," she said. She was standing close at my side
—so close that though she was not touching me, I sensed
the warmth of her body. " A few days ago the world to
me was just Pericele. I thought it would always be like
that. I could see no hope. And now——" She spread
her hands, embracing the sea and the rising light of the
moon that was already building a yellow path in our
wake.

I said, " I've a hunch that everything is going to be
all right now."

She nodded. " I think so," she said and laughed up
at me so that her eyes puckered and her teeth showed
white.

A hand gripped my arm. It was the Little Octopus.
He pointed his arm across the bows. The growing light
showed the smudge of an island crouched in the sea
ahead. " The Giglio," he said. " Within an hour you
should be homeward bound."

Behind us the moon topped the chain of the Apennines,
a great yellow cheese hung low in the sky. The sea was
suffused with an eerie luxuriant light.

" Come down to the cabin," he said, " and we'll have
a drink or two and discuss our plans."

I left Boyd on deck with Monique and followed him
and the captain. It was still hot down in the cabin and
cockroaches crawled across the flaking paintwork of its
wooden walls. It smelt of the food we had eaten for
supper and stale *vino*.

The captain tossed his greasy cap on to the table and
poured coarse red wine into tumblers. The Little Octopus
brought out a silver case and offered me a cigarette.
Engraved on the inside of the case were the initials G.D.R.
I caught his eye as I took a cigarette. Those were Del
Ricci's initials. His shoulders gave a slight shrug and
the corners of his lips turned down, as much as to say—
" That's the way life is if you live it that way." His eyes
were watching me with amusement.

He lit my cigarette for me with a lighter that matched
the case. His hand was quite steady. The captain lit

a long rank cigar. " Well, what's the plan ? " he asked.

It did not take us long to work it out. It was very simple. The L.C.T. was in Giglio harbour. The captain was to put the schooner alongside with a pretence at bad handling of his ship. As the crew of the L.C.T. came on deck they were to be either slugged or held up with fire-arms. There was to be no shooting unless things got out of hand. " It will all be very simple, I think," the Little Octopus said.

After that we had another drink. And then we went up on deck. As I put my foot on the companionway I felt the sweaty steel of a pistol thrust into my hand. " Just in case," the Little Octopus's voice whispered in my ear.

The island heights of the Giglio, castle-crowned, towered above the schooner now. And under what looked like a practically sheer slope a village crowded against the water's edge. This was Porto Giglio. The faces of the houses looked pale against the darker background of the hills and the church tower stood up like a sharpened pencil. We were under the lee of the land and the sea was calm like glass. Over the harbour wall a forest of schooner masts showed. And my heart leapt excitedly as I saw amongst them the squat stack and adobe-shaped bridge of the *Trevedra*.

Boyd had seen it too. He caught my eyes and raised his thumbs. I pointed it out to Monique and her eyes mirrored my own excitement.

We pressed back against the bulwarks whilst the crew hustled to lower sail. As the canvas slipped to the deck we rounded the arm of the harbour wall and made the entrance. And there, straight over our bows, the *Trevedra* rode at anchor in the very centre of the harbour. Squat and ugly and practical, she looked like an ungainly sea cow amidst all the beauty of the little moonlit port with its fishing schooners lying against the hard or pulled up for repairs on the sandy beach. She was low in the water which meant that she had a cargo.

" You'd better go below," I told Monique.

But she shook her head. " I do not want to miss the fight," she said.

It was astonishing to me that she really wanted to see a fight. Perhaps that was one reason why I was in love with her. She was so very different from most of the girls I had known. She had no veneer of civilisation. She was a strange mixture of the primitive and the innocent, and she had that naïve confidence in the world that is usually lost with childhood. And of course she was by force of circumstances dependent upon me. I had never had any one dependent upon me before.

My thoughts were interrupted by the Little Octopus's sharp voice giving orders. The captain's voice joined in and instantly there was pandemonium on the ship. Then the schooner shuddered as her bows struck the *Trevedra* at an angle as though trying to shoulder the heavy landing craft out of the way.

As the two vessels ground together, the *Trevedra* straining at her anchor chains, the crew of the schooner tumbled on to her decks with ropes and began to make fast.

A big man came down from the bridge. Two others appeared from the wheel-house. A heated argument began between them and the men from the schooner as to whether or not it was essential for us to moor alongside the landing craft. The Little Octopus, who was standing right beside me, watched the scene closely. I noticed how his own men were edging their way round behind the crew of the other ship.

Suddenly he put a whistle to his lips and blew a sharp low blast. Instantly his men produced black-jacks and slugged the two largest of the *Trevedra's* crew from behind. They slumped to the deck and the third man was still staring at them in astonishment when the butt of an automatic struck him down.

It was all done naturally and so easily. One minute there had been three husky men disputing the schooner's right to berth alongside. And now they were inert, lying like sacks on the rusty steel of the decks.

We went aboard then.

" 'Ome sweet 'ome," Boyd said. " I never thought I'd be glad to see a landing craft again. I wonder wot they've done with Jack and Mr. McCrae ? "

The Little Octopus took command now. He had the gangster's slickness in organisation. He posted Boyd and myself to the bridge and others to the various companion-ways. Then he stooped over the largest of the inert figures and slapped the man's face until he came to.

A lighter flame flickered, showing his face cruel and aquiline. Then the tip of a cigarette showed red. One of his men stuffed a rag into the man's mouth and then wound a handkerchief tight round his face so that he was effectually gagged.

I knew what he was up to and went down on to the deck. As I came up to the group around the squirming body of the man the smell of burning flesh was heavy in the night air.

I said, " What the hell do you want to do that for ? "

The Little Octopus swung round on me. " Shut up," he said. " And leave me to handle this my own way. You're getting your ship back, aren't you ? " The tip of his cigarette glowed and threw his face into red relief. Then he bent again and the man squirmed like a lobster dropped into boiling water, his whole body contorting to express his stifled screams.

Then suddenly the big face with the wide frightened eyes nodded.

His torturer straightened up and the gag was removed from the wretched man's mouth.

" Well ? " the Little Octopus asked.

" There is only Perroni. The two Englishmen are in the chain locker. They were alive when we battened them down."

" Where is Perroni ? "

But before the man could reply, there was a shout from the bridge. Boyd must have been caught napping. No doubt he had been watching the scene on the deck. As a result a thick-set man, whom I had no difficulty in recognising as the skipper of the *Pampas*, had him by the neck and was trying to throttle him.

The Little Octopus did not hesitate. He drew his pistol. I tried to stop him, but I was too late. A stab of flame, the soft plop of a silencer and Perroni jerked upright and rigid. Then he slowly keeled over and fell against the windbreaker of the bridge. The Little Octopus fired again and a hole appeared in the man's forehead and Monique cried out as she was splashed by the ugly pulp that spread over the back of the man's head, showing red in the moonlight.

" That's the lot then," said the Little Octopus to me. " I'll look after this. You go and get your two men out of the chain locker."

I felt slightly sick. It was so unnecessary—like burning that wretch with a cigarette end. But there it was. I called to Boyd to get Monique down off the bridge.

I met her at the foot of the port ladder. She was trembling like a leaf. Her hand slipped into mine like a kid that's got into a world it does not understand.

We went aft into the galley and down into the bowels of the ship's stern. Landing craft anchor from the stern and their chain lockers are therefore in a different place to other ships. We got the hatch of the locker up. I struck a match. It died for lack of air as soon as I thrust it through the hatch. But not before I had seen Stuart and Dugan, exhausted and wide-eyed, lying prostrate on the anchor chain.

" You all right, Stuart ? " I asked.

" It's you, is it, David ? " he said. " Thank God ! " His voice was thick and blurred. " We've been here two days." The Black Hole couldn't have been worse. The air was stale and smelt very bad.

I climbed through and got first Dugan and then Stuart up through the hatch. They were in a bad way. " No water. No food." Stuart explained painfully. Lack of air and the heat had done the rest. We carried them up into the fresh air and put them to bed in the bunks in the bridge housings. Monique brought water and then I told

Boyd to show her the galley and get some soup warmed up.

" Is the cargo all right ? " Stuart asked.

I nodded. " I imagine so," I said. " She's low enough in the water."

He smiled happily. " How did you manage to get here ? "

" The story will keep," I said. " It's none of my doing —just luck and the help of several people."

" I nearly gave you up," he said, and the water spilled on to the blankets as he sipped at the mug. " Thought you might think I'd welshed or something."

" I'm afraid we came pretty near to thinking that," I admitted. " We've been very lucky."

At that moment the Little Octopus walked in. " Arrivederci, Signore," he said. " I've cleared the remains from your bridge. I suggest you start your motors and get under way. The sooner you are out of here the better."

I said, " Stuart, this is the man who got the ship back from Perroni." Then to the Italian I said, " How can we repay you ? "

He shrugged his shoulders with an expressive lift of his hands. " It was a pleasure," he said. " Doubtless you will return to Italy. And some day I may need help. That is all I ask."

I was just about to thank him again when I noticed that Stuart had struggled into a sitting position. His eyes were narrowed dangerously. " Your name is Beni Jocomoni," he said. " The last time I saw you was up by Rimini nearly three years ago. You had just set fire to five houses in which you had locked the occupants. You were a partisan and on our side, but I would have shot you if you hadn't escaped through the smoke."

The Little Octopus turned down the corners of his lips. " Perhaps I am like this Beni Jocomoni. It is possible. But you are in no state, signore, to recognise people. It is a long time ago, three years. Much has happened. And at the moment I think you owe your life to me."

"Yes, I suppose so." Stuart slumped back on to the pillows. "But to have saved my life is small consolation to the innocent people who died to make a bonfire for your amusement."

The Little Octopus laughed and it was not a nice sound. "They would not give us food. Human life is cheap in a world where there is so much suffering. *Arrivederci, Signori.*" He bowed with a jerky theatrical movement of his slim body and went out through the door.

"I'll get under way," I told Stuart.

"Just a minute," he said. "What's happened to Perroni and Del Ricci? They caught us napping when we were alongside the mole waiting, fully loaded, for you to return."

I told him. And he nodded his head slowly, caressing his stubbly chin. Then he smiled a little wryly. "There's a certain strange justice about life, isn't there?" he said.

Monique came in then with some soup and I left him and went out on to the bridge. The schooner was casting off. I went down to the deck and thanked the skipper and his crew. He waved his hand and his engines began to go astern.

As the gap between the two craft widened something that reflected the moonlight flashed through the air and fell with a clatter at my feet. It was followed by another but lighter article. I picked them up. They were the silver cigarette case and the lighter that matched it.

The Little Octopus waved his hand in ironic salute.

I stood there and watched the schooner back out of the harbour entrance. Clear of the wall, her bows swung towards Elba. Her sails gleamed white as they struggled up to clothe her masts.

I threw the cigarette case and the lighter over the side. And as they sank through the clear sea water like silver fish I felt a sense of relief. I did not want to remember that particular facet of the expedition.

"Boyd!" I called. And when he came out of the galley I said, "Get the engines going, will you? I want to get out of here as quickly as I can."

"Aye, aye, sir."

I got a swab and went up to the bridge and washed all traces of Perroni's wretched end off the woodwork.

By the time I had swabbed the last of the blood the engines were going. Boyd and I got the hook up with the donkey engine and then I went up on to the bridge again and took the wheel in my hands.

"Slow astern both," I ordered.

"Slow astern it is, sir," came Boyd's report from the engine room and I felt the screws bite into the water and the ship begin to go astern.

As the harbour wall slipped past I ordered, "Full ahead, port—full astern, starboard."

The bows swung round. The little fishing village, white in the moonlight beneath the towering slopes of the island, revolved slowly round us and I headed the *Trevedra* along the rocky coast towards the open sea.

When we rounded the end of the island, I changed course, heading west for the Straits of Bonifacio between Corsica and Sardinia. I felt a strange contentment with the throb of the engines and the leap of the deck plates hard beneath my feet. I was my own master again. This was my ship and I was in command of her again. And I was homeward bound.

When the Giglio was just a dark mass astern beneath the great round disc of the moon and my wake was part of the silver path that led back to the island, Monique came out on to the bridge. She put her hand in mine, not afraid to touch me, and said, "I am glad that it is all right and that you have your ship again. You are happy, yes?"

She was looking up into my face, happy and child-like, yet with the eyes of a woman who understood my mood.

I slipped my arm round her and moved her body so that she stood against the wheel. Then I took her hands

in mine and put them on the spokes of the wheel, holding
them there beneath my own.

She leaned her body back against me and her hair was
on my cheek as she flung her head back to look up into
my face. She wasn't laughing now. She understood, and
her eyes were happy.

THE END